More prais

"A poetic rendition of survival under the conditions of war and occupation, this inspiring and passionate memoir is a reminder of the inseparability of the personal and political, and the local and global."
—Shahrzad Mojab, co-editor of *Violence in the Name of Honor: Theoretical and Political Challenges*

"Haifa Zangana proves once again that the act of writing can be truly liberating."    —Dalia Said Mostafa, research fellow, The University of Manchester

"In this powerful narrative, Haifa Zangana weaves a rich tapestry that portrays the repression, torture, and resistance in Saddam's Iraq against a complex social landscape. A must read for anyone who wants to understand Iraq today."
—Jacqueline S. Ismael, coeditor of the *International Journal of Contemporary Iraqi Studies*

Praise for *City of Widows: An Iraqi Woman's Account of War and Resistance*

"Zangana writes with indignation of the recent hijacking of her country."    —*Time Out New York*

"This angry, unforgiving and powerful book is as vital as it is hard to swallow."    —*Publishers Weekly* starred review

"What left me quaking was the power of internal perspective and history that she offers, and her informed explanations of both policy and practice."    —*Feminist Review*

# DREAMING

## HAIFA ZANGANA

# OF BAGHDAD

Translated from Arabic by the author,
with Paul Hammond

THE FEMINIST PRESS
AT THE CITY UNIVERSITY OF NEW YORK
FEMINISTPRESS.ORG

The Feminist Press at the City University of New York
The Graduate Center
365 Fifth Avenue, Suite 5406
New York, NY 10016
Feministpress.org

First Feminist Press edition

An earlier version of this work was published in English in 1990.

The "Big Brother" chapter was translated by Dr. Wen-Chin Ouyang.

Cover design by Faith Hutchinson
Text design by Drew Stevens

13  12  11  10  09    5  4  3  2  1

Library of Congress Cataloging-in-Publication Data

Zangana, Haifa, 1950–
  [Fi arwiqat al-dhakirah. English]
  Dreaming of Baghdad / Haifa Zangana ; translated from Arabic by Paul
Hammond and the author.
      p.  cm.
  Translated from the 1995 Arabic edition by Dar al-Hikma; originally
published in English in 1990 in France, under title Through the vast halls
of memory.
  ISBN 978-1-55861-605-9
  1. Political activists—Iraq—Nonfiction. 2. Women political prisoners—
Iraq—Nonfiction. 3. Torture victims—Iraq—Nonfiction. 4. Women—
Iraq—Nonfiction. 5. Iraq—History—1958—Nonfiction. 6. Baghdad
(Iraq)—Nonfiction. 7. Zangana, Haifa, 1950– 8. Authors, Iraqi—Biogra-
phy. I. Zangana, Haifa, 1950– Through the vast halls of memory. II. Title.
  PJ7876.A647F513 2009
  892.7′36—dc22

                                                                              2009003278

# CONTENTS

# FOREWORD

Haifa Zangana's *Dreaming of Baghdad* reads, sounds, and feels like drops of merciful rain. How many more books like this revelatory testimonial will we have, will we need, before the record is set straight—before we know what was Baghdad, whence Iraq, and who the Iraqis were before they were brutalized by the combined malignancies of Saddam Hussein and George W. Bush? Zangana's voice is at once elegiac and defiant, memorial and revelatory, sad but surreal in its visionary recital of what was and what might have been.

As a revolutionary activist Zangana was imprisoned and tortured by a tyrant, forced into exile, and made to watch in desperation as her homeland as she knew it was wiped off the map by George W. Bush. In these dark days, as she witnesses the destruction of her country, her prose is politically punctilious, an act of moral redemption—about a people she proudly calls hers and a homeland she inhabits with pride and poise. If the dastardly legacy of the Bush administration were to succeed in wiping out the entire collective conscience of the Iraqi people—along with monumental archives of their cultural heritage (in which resides the very alphabet of our humanity)—and all that remained was this beautiful rhapsody, the revolutionary defiance and the cosmopolitan culture she once lived could be deduced from it.

Zangana and I are almost the same age. She was born in 1950 and I in 1951, on two sides of Shat Al-Arab carrying our mutual memories of the Persian Gulf, the Arabian Sea, and the Indian Ocean. I read her and I relive the history of our two peoples (Iranians and Iraqis) through the loving reminiscences of my Iraqi sister. She speaks for both of our nations, brutalized, cut to pieces in body and soul. When I first met her in New York in November 2007, both of us were grayer than our green memories of the river that separated and united us in our youth. We both grew up under dictatorships, suffered the indignities of a democracy delayed, celebrated the aspirations we held sacred, and then saw the inferno of our two nations slaughtering each other to the delight of our enemies. When I read *Dreaming of Baghdad*, I couldn't help but wonder: why is it that Iran has not produced a Haifa Zangana in exile, but instead a platoon of self-sexualizing memoirists infantilizing a nation, whitewashing the harsh struggles of a people? My consolation: in Zangana's voice, there is a reverberation of her sisters in Iran, there is ample space for mine and ours. She speaks for both Iraqis and Iranians of her generation, men and women, and of a dream that was shared on both sides of that magnificent and generous river.

This book will teach you many things that the combined terror of Saddam Hussein and George W. Bush has forced an entire world to forget. It is impossible to imagine a timelier context for the publication of *Dreaming of Baghdad*. Against the backdrop of a self-promoting memoir industry Zangana stands out as a voice of a revolutionary Iraqi woman—tested, wise, and confident. She is the nightmare of Paul Bremer and his company, who have divided a deeply cultivated culture along sectarian lines to rule it better.

But erstwhile military governors or strategists are not the only arbiters of public debate about Iraq who will be deeply troubled by what Zangana writes in her book. In conjunction with the US-imperial apparatus that has invaded and conquered Iraq, an army of embedded anthropologists has now cornered the market of writing *about* Iraqi women. Haifa Zangana does not write *about* Iraqi women. She is an Iraqi woman. And her voice—clear, compelling, confident, and rebellious—speaks more voluminously and eloquently than libraries of ethnographic monographs and their prosaic theories. With the stroke of one magnificent act of literary courage and imagination she exposes the embedded anthropologists and their shameless mutation of a people into objects of ethnographic curiosity for their conquerors. Ever since the US-led invasion and occupation of Iraq, Iraqis have been robbed not just of their life, liberty, and national sovereignty, but above all of their right to represent themselves. In one travesty after another, US- and EU-trained anthropologists (especially those who don an Arab name or a distant Iraqi lineage) dismiss the experience of Iraqi women who have suffered under the military occupation as inauthentic and have the audacity to claim that right of representation for themselves. In *Dreaming of Baghdad* we meet and recognize Iraqi women for who and what they are, restoring dignity, pride, agency, and power to their voices. How poorer the world would have been without Zangana's courageous testimony. Without it, we would be at the mercy of the anthropologist doing fieldwork under the protection of the US Army, or the memoirist sitting in the shadow of the CIA in Washington DC, to report on Iraqi or Iranian woman.

Behold Haifa Zangana's act of revolutionary faith: here she speaks truth to power. "As we resist the occupation now," Zangana declares on behalf of her people, "our message is clear: We did not struggle for decades to replace one torturer with another."

Hamid Dabashi
New York City
May 2009

# DREAMING
## OF
# BAGHDAD

# PROLOGUE

I wrote this book in tiny installments over eight years, when I had persistent nightmares about my past. I was writing about my life as a radical activist in Iraq in the 1970s. I wrote it at a time when I didn't want or wasn't able to deal with memories of what had happened to me in prison. I wrote it while I was living in exile, missing my family terribly, believing I would never return to live in Baghdad again. I wrote it during the Iraq–Iran war, at the height of Saddam Hussein's popularity in Iraq, Arab countries, and the West. I wrote it in first person, as a record of my memories, and in third person, as I often saw myself, as if I were standing outside of my own life, trying to remember things and events as correctly and completely as possible. I wrote it with the hope that I would not betray the memories of the people with whom I worked or was imprisoned. I wrote it about her—not always about me—because I wanted to avoid the illusion of self as the center of events or history.

This may be the first published book written by an Iraqi woman to address the experience of imprisonment and struggle against the Baath regime, which lasted from 1968 to 2003.

Day after day, page after page, I gazed at my life fifteen years earlier, the life of a young woman with a Kurdish father and an Arabic mother. I was born in Baghdad and brought up in a middle-class family, destined to be either a doctor or a pharmacist. Instead I chose to be politically active. I joined a group of revolutionaries dreaming of a better Iraq for everyone regardless of their religion, race, or political belief. As a result I was arrested, imprisoned, and tortured. I was moved from Qasr al-Nihaya, the detention center for political prisoners, to Abu Ghraib, the general prison, to Al-Za'afaraniya, a prison for prostitutes.

In writing this book, I tried my best to document a decade of revolutionary struggle by a group of people who rebelled against the oppressive regime in Iraq. To put it another way, I tried to write about the lives and deaths of a group of young people who were able to foresee the horrible damage that the Iraqi regime was inflicting on its people long before the First and Second Gulf Wars. We were able to see beyond the present and predict the imminent deterioration of Iraq, despite its resources and huge oil wealth. Or maybe because of that. Everything around us indicated our own inevitable demise, but we tried. The future was the daily preoccupation of our revolutionary struggle. In writing this book, I felt I was paying a debt long overdue to my friends.

I also wrote this book to tell of my experience with torture. To break the silence. Silence becomes your refuge from the shame and guilt you feel for being alive. How do you talk about humiliation? About weakness and the fear of letting yourself and others down? About being reduced to an animal sleeping with urine and feces? Thirty years later I still often wake at two a.m., the time when they used to lead me out of my cell for interrogation.

Torture has left a deep scar on our collective memory, and death by torture was not an unusual fate for radical activists in Iraq. We wanted to put an end to this but we failed. The war and occupation in 2003, apart from shuttering Iraq as a country and people, has brought about many more imprisonments, many more deaths. Abu Ghraib is only one of many symbols. In occupied Iraq, torture became an instrument of humiliation and a way to force a nation into submission. As we resist the occupation now, our message is clear: We did not struggle for decades to replace one torturer with another.

On a personal level, writing this book in the 1980s was my way to gain courage to look at the past, record it, examine its values and mistakes, and to recapture its happy memories. In the process I liberated myself from my pain, sadness, disappointment, shattered dreams, and obsession with time past. Writing helped me to return to the present, to celebrate life without fear, and to regain joy and human feeling.

# CORRESPONDENCE

Dear Haifa,

I arrived in London a month ago. This city is gray, gray. My first observation about the English is that they are trained to look straight ahead; they are so involved in their private lives that they ignore the person next to them. How I wish I could find a haven where I could settle down forever. Sometimes I feel real joy. It is the beginning of the evening.

Will we ever return to live with the people we love, the ones whom we have lost? Here there is much harshness, little love. My room is small and I share the kitchen and bathroom with others. My young neighbor insists on leaving her dog locked indoors all day, and, as I am the only unemployed person in the house, I have to listen to its constant barking.

In a hopeless gesture to dispel the grayness of the weather, the walls, the furniture, the coats, and the briefcases, I have secretly painted my room red and black. The result: anguish of a different kind. Lying on my bed in the center of the room, I spend hours and hours watching TV.

I might apply to one of the Arab newspapers or magazines for work as a correspondent; that would help me sort out the visa problem.

Dear Haifa,

For years I believed I was immune to emotion, nostalgia, and dreams of returning to the places of my childhood. Now I am sitting here alone in the room I have just finished painting red and black, surrounded by books, papers, and a few paintings and posters, waiting apprehensively for the next news bulletin on TV. Yes, after the ads, the newscaster will read a few items about the Iran-Iraq war. They will show footage in which both sides in the conflict will claim victory. What we will see for the next few years are the images of men stepping over corpses, all smiles for the cameras. High and mighty is the rifle! Glory to the victory of death!

What a silent city! A city crowded with soldiers, dead sons, husbands and fathers, a city that insists on its own silence. But I am lucky, I tell myself and others, lucky to have left my own country years ago with a residue of human feeling intact. I feel happy and sad simultaneously. These are included in my plague of emotions: longing for the family house; longing to sit with the family at the table at dinnertime; longing to wander aimlessly through streets and alleys; to count the columns in Al-Rasheed Street, the main street in Baghdad which is crowded with passersby, cars, and peddlers; to watch a laborer uncover a shrine of an imam,* as he commences some long-delayed maintenance work. This is the face of my plague of emotions: a parade of ghosts wearing uniforms and sharing one body, chanting *glory to death* as they raise their hands in salute in unison. Against such a backdrop, does color have meaning? Do words have meaning? What has happened to our childhood friends? Why do we feel so anguished when we know the danger of standing on the edge of a cliff?

We creep back to our country quietly, one after the other, imagining that people are the same as when we left them, that the places are the same, that even the date palms are the same. And even the silence is the same. Silence and the persistent fear of others, no matter who. The children of this country of soldiers and the dead fix me forever with their gaze.

* "A holy man" in Arabic.

I pace round and round in my room, throw the book I am reading aside. Round and round a room whose total area does not exceed three square meters. I listen to the dog barking. Art during wartime is nothing but a safety valve. I think about how artists continue to work regardless of their art's lack of immediate impact. The body's defense mechanism says, Stand aside and smile bitterly. Thus the distanced observer can smile when the long-distance runner loses the race.

Dear Haifa,

Often our questioning leads us into endless corridors. Our questions resemble magical keys to a gate that leads to another gate, continuing ad infinitum. Childhood is always the question, and the logical answer is adulthood. The mind is boundless, and it is the greater part of life. It is an area where no human can plant his country's flag and say, This is my land.

Regarding the reasons for our failure, I do not agree with you. Lack of an opposition is not the problem, but its dissolution.

Fear is our friend and comrade; we grew up with it. It is closer to us than anything else. We have lived so long with fear, we cannot live without it.

How tired we are of moving from country to country, endlessly choosing between submission and submission.

This morning I received a letter from a friend who now lives in Sweden. He writes, "My heart bleeds when I remember my country. I am very tired. Do you know I have fond memories of the *goulnaz* flower? My father used to like its transparent red color, and when he died I tended the flowers in our garden. For two years, I have lived far from home, garden, flowers."

I feel exhausted from not sleeping for nights, always pursued by the same dream. It has become so familiar that I call it my recurring dream. I might send you details of it in my next letter.

Dear Haifa,

Here is my recurring dream: All of a sudden, I find myself in an airport I left years ago. I panic and feel sick. Here is my body recognizing fear before fear reaches my brain, recognizing images of torture, stored not in memory but in my body's cells. My heart palpitates and I think: When will they stop staring at me? How can I hide the trembling of my body and the pallor of my face? My body commences to claim its natural rights, to pass water, for example. I have undoubtedly taken the wrong plane. I was on my way to Madrid. How did I get here?

A man approaches me, and then another, and another. The circling is becoming tiresome. My teeth chatter and, without thinking, I smile, apologizing for a crime I have not committed. I smile at everybody, at the same time searching for a familiar face. Although all the faces are familiar, I cannot recognize one. The interrogation starts. Questions are asked, first by one person, then by others, all of whom are like students trying to outdo each other.

Why are you back? When did you leave? Why didn't you come back before? Where do you live? Who are your friends, your family, your relatives? I am so frightened I can't answer, so the crowd becomes aggressive, believing I am refusing to cooperate. Where is . . . ? What have you . . . ?

It's a dream . . . it's a dream. Soon I'll wake up. Calm down and you'll find yourself in bed. I can't breathe so I push the nearest man away.

I want to breathe . . . air. Another man replaces the first. I push him away. Another one replaces him. I remain in one spot, frightened, trembling, about to suffocate. I start screaming. Horror! I lose my sense of wholeness. Such fear rising in my body! My hands, eyes, lungs, and feet. And I start to run through the streets, avoiding looking back, swearing not to return to that place, even in my dreams. What do you do if inside you have a wound as big as yourself? What do you do if the wound inside you is your very existence?

Somewhere I read this sentence, but can't recall the writer: I am leaving but I promise to return when I am master of darkness and light. Do you know who wrote it?

Dear Haifa,
I know that my city, Baghdad, is dark. Even during the day, frightened women say, "Why is it night?" A sleepy man says, "I will sing for the love I long for."

I know that the inhabitant of the city is a sailor carrying his kit bag, ready to escape. I know that the statues in all its plazas are for but one man. Yet deep down in my heart is the longing, the yearning for a moment when the sailor will put down his kit bag, relax, and gaze happily at children's drawings empty of weapons and soldiers.

Dear Haifa,

Once again I go back to painting, feeling apprehensive, as if I am about to cross another shore. I was asked by a girl I met a few days ago, What about heritage? Why don't you paint what represents your heritage? I was taken aback by the question. I thought, didn't she look closely at my paintings? Didn't she see the human being with head bent, with limbs amputated, surrounded by walls? I replied, Heritage is a coffin we are forced to carry on our shoulders, then asked to run with on unfamiliar, rugged land. The coffin carries a warning: fragile, handle with care. My main concern now is to rework the painting so that it conveys my feelings. Hence my decision, like many other Iraqi artists, to make abstract painting. It is a way to distance ourselves from the nightmares and delusions we have inherited over the years.

Could that decision also be a step toward dialogue with the West? Western artists have been through the same dilemma. Painter Max Ernst said, "A horrible futile war had robbed us of five years of our existence. We had experienced the collapse into ridicule and shame of everything represented to us as just, true, and beautiful. My works of that period were not meant to attract but to make people scream."

Is sadness the first and last resting place? Is it the element that shatters dreams? Agony, stay away and let people wander through the forests of their dreams. At the end of the corridor stands a girl talking to the sun about her fear of darkness, raising a finger, entreating each and every one of us, Is it not time to restore to hope some of its glory?

ZINO

Zino was a long muddy road surrounded by houses built of rock brought from the mountains nearby. In the village there were a number of alleys starting at the muddy road and ending at the foot of the rugged mountains. The main road in the village was narrow, not because of any error in the original plan, but owing to the shopkeepers' persistence in displaying half of their wares outside. Thus sacks of rice, wheat, and barley sat beside children's clothes, rubber shoes, fabrics, sewing needles, and cotton, together with heaps of old magazines, religious and Marxists tracts in Arabic, Persian, and Turkish, with a few publications in Kurdish. In small wooden boxes were knives, forks, spoons, and kitchen utensils. Next to these were all kinds of pills, including painkillers and pills to combat indigestion. Believing Zino to be a popular resort, visited by thousands of tourists daily, the shopkeepers insisted on exhibiting postcards and local handicrafts. Each day at five p.m. (unlike other places, night visits Zino early), the shopkeepers hauled their goods back into their shops, waiting to re-exhibit them the next morning. Zino women were always in a hurry. On them fell the responsibilities of looking after husbands and children, sewing, tapestry, and weaving. Bedspreads had to be ready for winter. Little pieces of material were carefully collected and arranged in beautiful patterns for young brides. Women had to gather wood from the mountains and load it on the backs of mules, or their own backs if they had no mules. They helped their husbands farm and build temporary summer huts made from leaves and branches in the hope of renting them to tourists.

Because of the village's location on the Iraq-Iran border, one profession dominated village life: the black market. Zino was a free zone under the control of no government. The men carried the most modern weapons, and from time to time the women wore expensive jewelry. Trafficking included everything: weapons, carpets, fabrics, ammunition, hunting guns, fishing rods, leather belts, books, American toys, boxes of chocolates, packets of tea. After midnight, the men headed for the distant mountains, riding their mules or walking on foot across the border and returning with items for sale.

In the daytime, the village road was crowded with salesmen, black marketers, mules, and builders carrying their loads of stones. Children played in the street while old women looked on from their doorways. Houses in Kurdistan were not built all at one time. A family started by building one room and the toilet and kitchen, then added another room whenever they had the money, resuming work with the help of their neighbors. Sometimes the new room, with its low, unfurnished walls became a refuge for dogs. Fitting windows and doors was a task that took months because the materials had to be brought from a distant city. Openings for windows and doors remained empty during this time, and children would climb in through them when they got home from school, their cloth satchels full of books and pencils.

I was eight years old when my father took me with him to Zino to visit our Kurdish relatives. He was so proud to see me reading and writing Arabic that he never taught me his mother tongue, Kurdish. And although he was fluent in Kurdish, Persian, and Assyrian, Arabic eluded him.

We arrived in the village at noon. The road was empty and the shops were open with half their contents outside on the street. It was the time for prayer, lunch, and siesta. We headed for a half-built house, passing an incomplete fence, and walked through a room with no door or window. As we reached a wooden door, Mam* Mahmoud opened it, welcoming and hugging my father and me.

The room was almost empty except for a huge wooden box in one corner. On it there were blankets, cotton covers, and round pillows. From the other corner came the smell of tea brewing in a samovar and the scent of burning coal. I was fascinated by a beautiful, multi-colored Persian rug which gave the room a warm, welcoming atmosphere.

A few minutes later, Mam Mahmoud's wife, Mam Jin, walked in carrying a tray with four tea cups. She put it beside the samovar and shook hands with my father, then hugged me. Since I could understand very little of what they were saying in Kurdish, I occupied myself by watching cubes of sugar dissolve in my tea, which I stirred continuously, making enough noise to attract the adults'

* "Uncle" in Kurdish.

attention. I expected my father to be angry, as he would have been at home. Instead he remained silent and relaxed, sipping his tea as if time had lost its importance.

In that room, my father's presence was different from how he seemed in the city. He questioned Mam Mahmoud about our relatives and what they were doing, and he talked about the city. Mam Mahmoud talked about problems with border guards, and how times had changed.

Mam Jin was silent most of the time. When she spoke, she asked my father to make an appointment with a gynecologist for her. Mam Mahmoud was silent until finally he commented that it was getting late. I whispered, "Why can't we stay in Zino?" Noticing the way my father sat, and looking into his green eyes, I could see what it meant to come back to a place where he could stretch out, touch familiar things, and feel safe. I felt the urge to touch him, to make sure it really was him, the man who was lost to me in the big city. He sensed my feeling and stroked my hair tenderly. I whispered, "Why can't we stay here?" He did not reply. Living in Baghdad had been his dream, as being married to an Arab woman had been. Being proud of a daughter excelling in her studies was also his dream. "The cold weather has arrived early this year," said Mam Mahmoud as he quietly stepped outside, on the lookout for the last birds of summer. He walked ahead of us toward one of the shops, which, unlike the rest, was locked up. He unlocked the door, and from the darkness within came an unforgettable smell. In the years that followed, and in moments of despair, the memory of that smell became for me a window opening to the sky. It was the smell of darkness, humidity, and mounds of Persian carpets rolled up in a certain way to keep them safe from moths. I jumped on them, and as my father gave instructions, I helped Mam Mahmoud pull one out. He unrolled the carpet in front of the shop. How beautiful it was! I stood there gazing at the endless patterns of bright colors with fascination. Moving closer, I felt the wooly texture and tried to imitate and upstage my father in savoring its smell. Mam Mahmoud laughed and hugged me again. We bought two carpets that day. Then we started our journey back to the city.

# BAGHDAD

I was twenty years old. I stood in the middle of a room in front of four men. My boxes of books and pamphlets, a huge desk, recording machines, and a sofa were against one of the walls; leftovers of a meal remained on a tray. The man sitting behind the desk did not say much. His name was Nazim Kazar, and he was the head of the Iraqi secret intelligence. He was of medium height with dark skin, and wore sunglasses with gold rims. He had on a dark suit and held a rosary. He divided his attention equally between it and me, as if debating something.

He was lord and master of the palace Qasr al-Nihaya, the detention center for political prisoners in Iraq. He knew everything that took place within its four walls. He received visitors and delegated them to various rooms. While the government was maintaining its façade of civility and the Communist Party's main opposition was busy polishing a few bricks in the hope of securing a couple of seats in the government, this man had absolute freedom in arresting, torturing, and executing detainees in the labyrinth of that castle.

Four years later, at noon on a hot, sunny day, the master of the palace, Nazim Kazar, suffered

the same fate: he was arrested, tortured, and executed by his own government.

What was to become of me? One of the men
prowled around me, and then touched me. As he
did so, I could hear the laughter of the other men
in the room. I was so scared, I had no time to be
disgusted by the slimy hands touching my body.
I looked at the curtains, the walls, the boxes of
books, and, as I smiled stupidly, the man hit me
across the face, his coarse words swirling around
my body. When he hit me on the head, lights
danced in front of my eyes. I was pushed against
a wall. The master, who so far had remained calm
and silent, now moved for the first time and told
his men to leave me alone. Approaching me, he
pointed to my clothes, and I quietly put them on.
He told me to sit beside him, and asked me softly,
"Are you hungry?"

"I want to go to the toilet."

One of the men accompanied me to the toilet
on the first floor, which was not an easy task, as he
had to stop me time and again and order me to face
the wall as other prisoners filed by. After they had
gone, there were drops of blood on the ground. I
followed the man to the first floor and he showed

me to the toilet. No, it was a just a room with a tub. I turned around, confused. He said, "What's the difference? Do what you want to do here," and he stood behind me. I urinated and returned with him to the hall.

There the master asked me to sit next to him and eat dinner. "And now . . . I want you to tell me everything you know." He patted me on the shoulder tenderly as if he were a friend I had not seen in a long while, and all he wanted was to hear my latest news.

"About what?"

"It doesn't matter. Tell me about anything."

Remain silent for two days. Those had been my instructions. After that, people would get to know about my arrest, meetings would be canceled, hiding places would be changed. Two days of silence: this was the lullaby I comforted myself with, and a smile coursed through my shivering body. The master of the palace stood up and said, "It seems you are all alike. I thought you were an intellectual with nothing in common with those ignorant people."

He left and I did not see him again. For a while, I was alone. The palace was very quiet. The thumping of my heart eased off; I began to think of the others, something I had done my best to avoid until then. Suddenly the door opened, and a short little man entered, followed by four henchmen. With his bulbous eyes he supervised everything that took place in that room and thoroughly enjoyed the moans and screams of the tortured. Four years later, at noon on a very hot day, that little man called Hassan Al-Mutairy went through the same tribulations; like the master of the palace, he was arrested, tortured, and executed by his own government.

He looked at one of his men, who then left the room and returned with a fellow officer, dragging in a prisoner. The prisoner's head was swollen and covered in dried blood. The two men dropped him on the floor. I was surprised when the victim whispered my name, and then I recognized my friend, a friend of my family's. Here was a man my family loved, a man whose visits we eagerly awaited. We adored spending long hours listening to him at night, to the tales of his imprisonment and how all the comrades cared about him because he was the youngest, how his jokes helped people pass the time and forget their fears of interrogation and torture. He did not look towards me now; he was no more than a mound of flesh encrusted with dried blood. He confirmed my identity and then he was dragged out of the room. That was the last time I saw him. Two months later he was executed with two other comrades; one was twenty-three years old, the other sixteen.

Many others were brought into the room. All of them had been tortured and disfigured to the extent that I only recognized them by their voices. The room became smaller and smaller . . .

Was I going to tell him anything? Two days of silence were all I had to bear. I looked at him idiotically. Things happened so quickly I didn't have time to think. An exhausted looking man came in and began beating me and kicking me in the groin. My underwear was wet with blood and urine. Then someone kicked me in the head.

When I awoke I was in a small room, empty except for an old sofa. One of the windows faced a high fence; I must have been in the south wing of the palace. The floor tiles were stained with dried blood, which I tried to scrape off with the toe of my shoe and push to the other side of the room. Despite terrible pain, I kept on trying. There were people's names scribbled all over the walls. Realizing it was daytime, I knocked at the door. When at last it was opened, I asked permission to go to the toilet. The man told me to urinate in the room and locked the door quietly. I thought they must be busy with new detainees. New prisoners.

I spent two weeks in that room. On the second night, or maybe the third, and after the little man had stopped sending for me many times a day, I realized why the beatings had stopped: I must be their personal favorite, their current VIP. Then, on the third night, I heard screams like none I had ever heard before. Was it a human being screaming or an animal howling? It was a mixture of a human voice denying knowledge and a continual howling, interrupted by sudden screams, followed by a voice begging and pleading for mercy, followed by more screams.

For two weeks, I could not sleep. I listened by day for the torturer's steps to approach and take me to be interrogated again, and by night I tried to recognize the voices of the tortured, to discover who else had been arrested.

One day I was visited by the prison doctor, who gave me some antibiotics, and on another day by one of the torturers, who felt sorry for me when he saw both my legs and skirt were covered in menstrual blood. He gave me an old shirt which I cut into pieces and put between my legs. He grew more sympathetic and allowed me to go to the toilet, and finally handed me a broom and a bucket to clean the room of excrement and urine.

The men got used to my presence there and stopped ordering me to face the wall whenever they pushed another prisoner by. Once, while standing in a queue to go to the toilet, I stood behind a prisoner who was carrying a bucket of excrement and urine. The guard was annoyed because one of the prisoners was taking a long time in the toilet, so he ordered the prisoner with the bucket to throw its contents over the tardy comrade when he emerged. The torturers' laughter was louder than usual, their amusement endless. Ordering the prisoners to clean the floor, a guard led me back to my room, and I was deprived of going to the toilet at all that day.

While I was in the palace, I had the privilege of a visit. One of my influential relatives visited me for a few minutes. That meant my family knew I was alive, and they were trying to get me released. Indeed, if what my relative said was true, I was about to be released very soon. After two days, two men entered the room and ordered me to follow them. At the palace gate they stopped and blindfolded me. There my temporary elation ended. I sat between them in the back of a car, and we began our journey of many miles. Questions swirled in my head. From some of their comments, I inferred that they were taking me somewhere to execute me. Sitting stiffly, I thought that maybe I was already dead. Suddenly, I could not hear their questions and comments. I had no idea if the journey had lasted a few minutes or many hours. The car stopped. I burst into tears for the first time since my arrest. No, the journey was not to execute me, but to transfer me, thanks to my father's efforts, to Abu Ghraib, an ordinary prison.

I was released after six months, during which time I was moved again to a prostitutes' prison. I had become ill, my face covered in sores. I cried for any tender word or gesture. My hair began falling out. For a whole year afterwards, I was reduced to an entity closed in upon itself, absorbed in remembering that howling, remembering the dead.

# LONDON

At the airport, I anxiously awaited my father. What a fantastic thing it was to see him after so many years! I imagined him as I had left him in Baghdad: angry, threatening, and promising that everything would change within a few months. After years of waiting, he had come to visit me. But when he approached me, he cried bitterly. He was pale, and had lost his good looks. Illness and oppression had made him a habitual sufferer of fever, insomnia, and impotence. After many years of waiting, he had become a man who lived only to drink *arak** and consume huge quantities of pills. He was bitterly waiting for the final knock at the door. He said, "It seems as if they are everywhere. They only stay for a while, just long enough to accompany the chosen to their arrest. People now prefer to keep their faces to the wall. Happiness has lost its meaning." His sadness was conveyed by his questions: "What has happened to people? What has happened to me?"

I have a small flat and a good job. The window of my sitting room looks out over the city. The city's doors are open wide. And yet, after ten years, I am still hesitant to enter. I miss the past. I feel unfulfilled by my body, with wounds deeper than scars

* An alcohol similar to Ouzo.

can reveal. At night, I wake in fear, surrounded by blood and my friends' faces. I long for solitude, but I fear it, too. I long to look calmly into myself without interference from others. Yet I feel afraid to do this and so I stretch out my arms, searching for others' help.

Hugging my father, saying good-bye, I realized I would not see him again. Two months later, he died. The doctors said he refused to live.

In this darkness, in the solitude of waiting, I am seated with my eyes open, yielding to repetition, thinking once more of what happened. I have tried to forget that day. Burdened by the shining sky and the bright light, I begin to see things, minute details, that cannot remain hidden: old family photos, a morning interrupted by the joyful voices of children playing in an alley, familiar faces, friends I might meet if only I were not here . . .

I have not the slightest intention of lamenting a vanished childhood or searching for long-lost human warmth. But I will try my best to follow a friend's advice. He told me, always begin from the outside: get to the bottom of things, probe their depths, but always from the outside.

His advice reminded me of a warning given to me years ago by my teacher: You may, in future, go on to make a name for yourself. But somewhere, sometime, you will be faced with a choice... What choice? I interrupted. Without giving a response, he continued. When an individual is wholly creative, at one with her destiny, there is neither time nor space, life nor death.

I do not know what the link is between these two bits of advice, but even after twenty years, I feel resentment. Why didn't I learn to listen early on?

At two p.m., on the day of my arrest, I'm in the Bab Al-Mu'atham district of Baghdad. I see the lines of taxis broiling in the August heat. Their drivers have taken refuge in various cafes and restaurants and even under bus shelters, with crowds of women with children in one hand, empty bottles in the other. They are off to the children's hospital nearby. The bottles, which all patients must supply, are to be filled with prescribed medicines. Is it the heat wave or my own imagination that exaggerates this picture in my mind?

I cross the street to walk in the thin shade of the high prison walls. Despite the heat, I walk slowly to avoid tripping over my abaya. Yet I stumble again and again, cursing the need to wear an abaya on my travels to these country towns. I think, maybe I will be able to remove it when I go to the cemetery. The street is empty and I can hear the echo of my own footsteps. People are napping or moving quietly behind their curtains, as they usually do at this hour. I cross another street to walk in the shadow of another wall.

We are obsessed with building fences. Our children grow up, not in fields, but behind walls; they reach their prime of life cuddling walls that hide gardens, colorful lights, and fountains. Whenever we moved to a new house in my youth, my mother would insist on building the fence higher to keep us protected from prying eyes. With equal persistence, my brothers would bore holes in that fence to spy on our neighbors' daughters.

This wall, however, was different, though built of the same red brick used elsewhere. It was the wall of the Bab Al-Mu'atham cemetery. Half of the cemetery was in ruins, the other half full of palm trees. It was the breeding ground for stray dogs and cats. The afternoon we went to visit my grandfather's grave, I remember my mother explaining that the cats were so fat because they fed on freshly buried corpses. My grandmother immediately silenced her by saying that the cats thrived on aborted fetuses thrown to them at night by the nurses from the hospital nearby.

I remember, too, that the whole area had a peculiar smell, a mixture of orange blossom (there were orange trees on either side of the main street), roses, gardenias, and carnations placed in the Turkish martyrs' cemetery, and the phenol and antiseptic from the forensic laboratory, the school of pharmacy, and the old surgical and dental hospitals.

I saw the cemetery guard asleep, leaning in the shade against the wall. He excelled in nurturing palm trees. Every year he would employ one of the local peasants to prune them, and every year the trees produced the best-quality dates, which no one collected. Who would dare eat such fruit, thriving as it did in earth full of corpses?

Later, when I learned the rudiments of self-defense, when I learned how to kill, I wished we might be satisfied eating such dates.

Few of the barefooted children who ran by noticed my presence. Were they ghosts? Was I? Exhausted less by the heat than by daydreaming, I walked quickly, sweating and straining to reach the garden gate of my house. I wanted to relax in my room there, to sleep after so many days on the road going from town to town. I hoped to enter the house quietly, without waking anyone from their siesta. Opening the gate, I saw that the sitting room curtain was pulled back slightly. It twitched: the authorities were waiting for me. Why had I not rung to make sure everything was all right before returning? I threw my abaya and handbag down. Fear gripped me. I ran in hope that someone might help me escape. I felt all the instincts of an animal trying to survive. I did not dare look behind me. All I wanted was to reach the main street. Suddenly, one of my pursuers grabbed my braids. I froze, which surprised them. They were pointing their guns at me. I stood stock-still, tranquil, like a statue. I had often asked myself what I would do at such a moment. Every night I had hidden behind the thin curtain of sleep, memorizing roles of characters who were not me. I was the surprise element in the play.

What happened seemed not to concern me. I told my body to adjust itself accordingly, told it to remain firm, get a grip on my shaking limbs. But my mask-like face could not help betraying emotion. (It took my face years to regain its original mien.) Although surrounded by people, I was completely alone. When I told a friend much later what had happened, she remarked, "But you talk about it as though it happened to someone else!"

I now realize how true her remark was. The road was long. Did I know the way? I had reconnoitered it beforehand. The street, the silent house, the mysterious anxiety, the fears regarding a place I had never visited, the palpitating of my heart. I wish I could lock that heart in an embrace. O heart, calm thyself. Our consolation is that young people do not age in our city; the lifespan here is short. Dryness kills plants, and ordinary people kill animals as their way of venting anger. "Why?" the man sitting next to me asked. Surely he knew! It is for the challenge. We bear it, tamed by continual fear, within us, and we liberate it in moments of madness. What I did during those years was to celebrate the flames of a precious madness.

In the car I considered my luck. It appeared the driver was a very important person. The soldiers outside and inside the Qasr saluted him fervently. He stopped the car and told me to follow him. It was then I remembered my first visit to the Qasr at the age of seven. It was during the first days of the 1958 revolution. Originally built for the crown prince, the Qasr was opened to the public after the revolution. For a brief period, this grandeur belonged to the people. That day, I went with my mother, my two aunts, my grandmother, and my two brothers, all in our best clothes. I was wearing an uncomfortable pair of new sandals, which I complained about incessantly. Nobody took any notice because they were too busy looking, pointing, and whispering. I could not understand why we had to whisper. My grandmother at last took notice of my tears and said in a loud voice, "Be quiet, be quiet!"

"Why should I be quiet?"

Turning and scolding me, she replied, "We mustn't disturb the dead." Even in the jubilance of the moment, of our country's hard-won liberation, she could not forget what transpired here in the past.

The Qasr had beautiful landscaped gardens. In the front yard there were stables. They were later turned into cells by the new regime.

In August, the hottest month of the year, I felt cold.

He sat behind a huge desk in a spacious room whose furniture bespoke good taste. I could see my image in his heavy tortoise eyes—soft, vicious eyes that had drunk deeply at every well.

I have not forgotten that hour in twenty years. It comes to me now in the darkness, in the solitude of waiting, where I now sit. It is here that I see things that I have never glimpsed before, not fantastic objects as in dreams, but the most banal and commonplace things, seeing them as if for the very first time. I am not fit to be a hero or a victim.

"There is no choice," he said.

"What if I refuse?" I wondered.

I looked up, trying to grasp what I had seen. Was there any evidence, any justification for hope? Then they brought in my friends, one by one. All of them had tortured bodies and a strange emptiness in their eyes. They recited the well-rehearsed litanies like school children who had memorized a text. Everything around us emphasized the inevitable: death. Yet we tried. There was something in us, something we had built up together. I gathered my wits and listened carefully.

Then I was winched up to the surface of the world again. When I stepped out among my people, they recoiled. They turned away in silence. Since that day, I have lost my urge to scream. I have lost all joy and human feeling. I still possess all the old words, but nothing else.

I look at the past as it approaches, falling on me, enfolding me, as though in layer upon layer of concrete. I look in silence. I do not even try to protect my face with my hands. I want to scream. The scream has become a whisper: memory, draw closer. You, particles of concrete, do not sink into the lobe of the brain where memory resides, but spread all over into the lobes of the past, the future, sleep, sight, thought, happiness, sadness, passion. The past is the present is the future.

I recall various events. Even revised by memory, they remain unchanged, full of color, surprising to me. What I do now is recall the joyfulness of early days, the deep, intimate feelings, the innocent laughter. What I do now is look at my face in the mirror and see its pale, exhausted reflection, its skin which has lost its elasticity and which rarely smiles. An empty smile that resembles the emptiness of a spacious house that lacks the warmth of human presence. Gazing at my body, I see not limbs and torso, but a panel with colored buttons. I press the green button on the right each morning to go to work. I use the red button on the left to show courtesy. I use it to agree with other people, to repeat the word "yes." There is also a yellow button in the middle that I press each night before sinking into a comatose sleep. Over the years, I have managed to reduce my hours of waking. I take sleeping pills at six p.m. each day, the minute I get home from work. The dream I recall on awakening is always the same: it's about the past.

PORTRAIT

His life was short but rich, crammed with events. He was arrested at the age of seventeen, released five years later, and executed when he was twenty-four.

At the foot of the mountains, the bushes burn and the vines trod. Herbs are burning, villages are burning, huts of leaves and branches are burning.

Young men take refuge in caves. After the danger has passed, I hear his laughter. Has he ever stopped laughing?

I try now, as I have tried in the past, to forget his mutilated features as I saw them at our final meeting. I want only to remember his relaxed face with its smile directed at his comrades, his friends, his country.

When I first met him, the note I received was short and precise: "Fouad, three p.m., in front of the Iraqi Museum." I approached silently, three minutes late, after checking the rendezvous point twice to make sure he was the right person. He was of medium height and build, wearing a white shirt and a pair of gray trousers. His hair was red; his fair skin was reddened by the burning sun. He moved restlessly, though his face was relaxed. He was not carrying anything.

"Hello."

"Welcome."

Then silence. Since he was my superior, I awaited his orders. He walked quickly with short strides, and I could not keep up with him as he crossed the street. The unbearable heat made everyone seem tired, as if they were sleepwalking. I felt like that, too. I asked him sarcastically, "Why don't you run?"

He turned around as if he had only just noticed my presence, and laughed. I thought, at last, a comrade who can laugh and not feel guilty about it, or think his revolutionary image is threatened by levity. Perhaps it was because he had left school early and didn't consider himself an intellectual. He was arrested before he had had time to read Kafka's *The Metamorphosis*, Dostoevsky's *Crime and Punishment*, Camus' *The Outsider*, or even Colin Wilson's *Ritual in the Dark*. He retained his spontaneity.

When we were far from the crowd, he told me briefly that I would be in charge of certain activities: the students' union and the women's organization. I said I was willing to do whatever he ordered me to do. Then he suggested taking me to meet another comrade. We waited fifteen minutes for a bus. The heat was incinerating everything in the city. I could feel sweat running down my back and legs. Although few in number, passersby were unable to disguise their curiosity. A man and a woman standing together: how suspicious! At last the bus came. It was a double-decker and we went upstairs. A conductor followed us. In addition to their usual duties, bus conductors are guardians of public morals. Fouad wanted to pay both our fares, but I stopped him, saying he should pay his and I would pay mine. He looked at me incredulously, as did the conductor. A year later, Fouad laughingly reminded me of this, saying, "I was very pleased with your independence, but why did you refuse to pay *my* fare?"

The base was our home. As time wore on, there were fewer books to read, less hobnobbing in cafes, less time to sit together and endlessly chew words. Newspapers were scattered all about as we sang old songs; singing is often enjoyed at gatherings. Our voices were urgent, enunciating signals, images, and illuminations with but one dimension: the future. The future is our daily preoccupation. What is to happen? What will we do? What will our future society—our dream —be like? The future is our horizon. How vast will it be?

Fouad was arrested at noon on a hot day.

The heat had enough force to keep people in their houses. Noon was the ideal time for secret meetings, for making plans, but it also meant that if you were in trouble or about to be arrested, there was no one around to help. Two days before, I had met Fouad on my way back from Kurdistan. He told me two of our comrades had been arrested, and advised me to keep a low profile for a while. As for him, well, he had to leave Baghdad for Kurdistan. His presence in the city was too dangerous for him and his comrades. He was sad to have to leave the base. He wanted to remain in the city he considered the center of his life and political activities. When I told him how sad he looked, he made himself regain his cheerfulness. After all, he said, this would be an ideal way to rid himself of Baghdad's heat and dust.

I looked at him with deep sadness that day. Had I, too, caught the germ of anguish? Would this moment remove the veil of our real emotions? I looked intently at his face, trying to engrave his features into my memory. In this, I succeeded. I, who can sit for hours trying to recall the features of a close friend, have no such problem with Fouad's. Sometimes I try to forget, but I fail. Was he handsome? I do not think so. But his presence was calming, even to those who had only just met him. Often they would leave wondering where they had met him before. A first meeting with him was like picking up an interrupted conversation with an old friend.

I did not know then that it would be the last time I would hear his laugh. When he was arrested, he was on his way back to pick up his suitcase from a friend's place. He did not foresee any danger. He had the false sense of security of a man who is paying his last respects to his city. His instincts failed him, this man who regularly traveled from city to city, refuge to refuge, base to base. He walked naively into their trap. The security men were waiting. They had to gun him down. That hot summer's day, Baghdad's back alleys witnessed four men chasing and shooting at a young man who thought he knew his beloved city as well as he knew himself. He fired back before collapsing to the ground, covered in blood. A week later, one of the Qasr al-Nihaya torturers pointed to his own bandaged head and arm and said, "One of your party's bastards did this." He was pointing to Fouad's final protest.

"Sit down."

"Thank you."

"Are you hungry?"

"No."

"Do you want something to drink?"

"No."

"Now, since you are comfortable, tell us everything you know."

"I don't understand."

"I already know your answer. You are all the same at the beginning."

He sighed with boredom, revealing how tired he was with my stubbornness.

"Let her confront the others."

My interrogator signaled to the man standing at the door to let the first terrorist in. They brought in a disfigured mass of flesh, carried by two men as if it was not able to support itself. I recognized the torn clothes covered in blood and filth. The confrontation was brief, but I recognized

Fouad's voice. He did not look at me; perhaps he was avoiding my face, or maybe he could not see properly. He did not say much except to confirm my identity and acknowledge our connection.

I think now, as I always have, that when I die, I will take with me something of this world. That thing will be the image of Fouad's tortured body. The image of a young man transformed in ten days into a mass of unseeing, unhearing flesh. The image of an idealistic, beautiful dreamer disfigured by torture.

Three months later, Fouad and two of his comrades were executed. Before his execution, at Abu Ghraib, he managed to send me a note: "My dear neighbor, I have been in the death cell for two months. They have allowed my family to see me, as I shall be executed very soon. How are you? Best wishes, and don't laugh at my spelling mistakes."

Now, whenever I meet comrades who survived, they are burdened like me with the guilt of still being alive. We spend our evenings talking of the past. I address them as if they are not there, and they talk about me as if I am somewhere else. They speak of a girl in her twenties. I talk about them as young men. The only living presence among us is the past. "What has happened to . . . ? Do you remember . . . ? I wonder if . . . is still alive?" These repetitive questions underline our feelings of exile. We see each other through a thin veil, an unremovable veil. We stretch out our arms to push away our past lives, our faces, but they stay where they are. The questioning is a new habit we have acquired. Will we be able to create ourselves afresh, behave in a different way, rekindle our dreams? Will we ever again enjoy the life we learned of in school, lessons the authorities then tried to make us forget? Will we play similar roles in similar cities in different times?

Until now, history has striven to repeat itself by rotating around a single axis: humans. Is there any guarantee that we, too, will not wear the faces of the torturers in the future?

# NAWCHILICAN

Y ou stand here and I'll guard the other side of the base."

When she heard his voice, invested with such authority, she almost saluted him, saying, "Yes, sir!"

Do particles of darkness add extra dimension to the human voice?

In the distance she saw faint light emitted by small windows. She saw a ghost move. Who would like to walk alone on a night like this? Although she was wearing two pairs of socks, her feet were cold. She stood up and walked a few paces to the right to avoid Saad, the second guard. Her coat was big and heavy; she was carrying it rather than wearing it. It was Abas's coat; he had felt sorry for her and had given her his, after first telling her its history:

> Last summer Kaka* Kawa, one of the local farmers, came to the base asking for the doctor. As you know, we don't have a doctor, but since I know some first aid, I pulled myself together and offered my services, hoping that the problem wasn't serious and

* "Brother" in Kurdish.

I could treat it with the little medicine we had. But if it was serious, I'd have to take him to the hospital. He told me it was his daughter he was worried about. I asked him to speak slowly because my Kurdish wasn't good. Apparently his daughter had suffered from diarrhea for three days. This is easy enough, I thought, a common enough complaint. With the firmness of a real doctor, I told him to stop giving her food for twenty-four hours and make her drink as much fluid as she could, especially boiled water. A month later, Kaka Kawa came to the base asking for Dr. Abas. He shook my hand in gratitude and pulled a coat from the sack he was carrying. He said his eldest brother had brought it back after participating in an attack on the army. The soldiers had fled, leaving their belongings behind. The coat was one of theirs.

Rubbing her hands together to warm them, she wished she could talk to the other guard, but how could she talk to him when Saad resented her very presence on the shift?

The shapes of the mountains were strange in the dark. The darkness, too, seemed strange. It was pitch black, yet she could make out the distant mountains, as if they were women wearing black abayat. The murmur of countless streams made up their voices. How many streams there are in Kurdistan, she thought, and how abundant and mysterious they are! They water the fields and the pastures. They are the refuge of fish and ferns. Here the water is cold in summer; there, hot in winter. Trees and grass and people thrive on the banks. But then the streams were obliterated by order of the ruler of the country. His orders were immediately put into effect and the beautiful springs of Kurdistan were stopped up with concrete. Silence ensued.

The guard's face was pale. Most faces at the base were pale. Food was scarce. Their pharmacy was so primitive, she spent hours checking the expiration dates of the medicines they had. In the end, she had to discard most of them. Dr. Abas looked at her suspiciously.

"Are you sure you know what you're doing? We've waited such a long time to get them."

When she complained about the filthiness

of the main room used for meeting, eating, and sleeping, when she mentioned that its smell was unbearable and that cleaning the place was not so difficult (since all they had to do was spread the mattresses outside in the fresh air), they looked at her as if she was an alien from outer space. Most of them ignored her remarks, but a few sympathized.

"Comrade, this is a fighters' base, not a bourgeois sitting room." Bourgeois, bourgeois—how she hated that word! How is it possible that a mere word can cover a multitude of sins?

In a stormy argument with Abu Jaffar, a senior member of the Politburo, and with Abu Samira, who was in charge of the base, Abu Jaffar said in his usual mocking voice, "The guards must be as alert as falcons and as quick as gazelles . . ." He ceased speaking without finishing his thought. Was he about to ask her if she possessed these qualities? The day before, she was not allowed to approach the village nearby, she was told, "because you are the only woman among us."

"But I am not the only woman! There is Um Jaffar* as well."

* Um means "mother of" in Arabic. The fighters spoke both Arabic and Kurdish.

"That's different! Um Jaffar is with her husband and children in the house by the *rubar*.*"

"But the villagers know them."

"Yes, but your case is different. We have to respect the villagers' way of thinking, and imagine the rumors your presence would provoke . . ."

"Why do you say that?" she screamed, taking him aback.

"You are a girl, a girl!"

"I'm telling you, I'm your comrade before anything else!"

She stubbornly refused to heed him, and the argument grew more irritating until Abu Samira intervened and sided with her. Abu Samira was the base's peacemaker; whenever there were arguments or problems, he was called immediately. The solution, according to Abu Samira, was to have two guards instead of one. She was blind with rage, a rage that would accompany her during her time at the base, while she delivered weapons to other bases in the South, during her relocation from place to place, and when she was arrested and tortured. An anger so strong that she lost the

* "Stream" in Kurdish.

ability to argue or even to speak. She remained silent, like an idol that had once known what it was like to be surrounded by worshippers, to be the recipient of sacrifices.

They could feel the weight of her anger.

She kicked a stone, then a frozen branch. Corpses are well preserved under the layers of ice. Death. What is death? We meet it so often, yet know little about it. And each time it wears a different face. They say it is the demise of living cells. They say it is the end of mental life, the departure of a soul for another body, another shell. Is it, then, a mere exchange of containers? It must be easier to understand than fear. Fear paralyzes limbs and deprives humans of trust and love. She recognized death at various moments. It made faces change, caused wrinkles to dominate features, line upon line beneath the eyes, at the corner of the mouth and forehead.

"Have you slept?"

"No. I was thinking."

"What about?"

"If we're attacked, what will we do?"

"We will wake the others and warn them."

His voice was deep, his words precise.

Three years later, Saad was arrested. In Qasr al-Nihaya, he went mad and was transferred to a mental hospital. When he was released, he collaborated with the secret police, helping them identify and arrest his comrades.

How many hours until morning? She longed for a cup of tea. One step, two steps, then she turned to sit on a rock near the mouth of a cave that overlooked the street. The cave was used as a kitchen. Nearby were ghee tins, scrubbed clean and used to bring water from the *rubar* nearby, where Abu Jaffar and his family were staying.

During her visit to Nawchilican, she had met scores of fighters. Some of them stayed permanently at the base, others, like herself, came for a brief period, either to be trained in soldiering or to bring weapons and leaflets and receive instructions. Nawchilican was a place full of enthusiasm, dreams of a new life in a country enveloped in mist. Nawchilican was a source of light that attracted young people yearning to reawaken the beloved children inside themselves. They left their houses and jobs, colleges and schools, lands and fields, and headed for the liberated zone. There they began to plant, teach, publish, fight, and write down their dreams of a better world, a better tomorrow. They asked those who came to the base about their families, especially their mothers. Fathers have long memories and do not easily forgive. Their anger takes longer to subside.

She met mothers who had slipped out of their houses to inquire about their sons. One mother, Um Khalid, asked her, "My son, how is he? Who cooks his meals?"

"Nobody. He cooks for himself and for the others."

"Who washes his clothes?"

"No one. He washes his own and has learned to make bread."

She laughed loudly, remembering how the comrades teased this mother's son about his bread, "strong as a good pair of shoes." The mother was not amused; she looked at her in a way that froze her laughter instantly. The mother thought her son was the best man in the world. If he learned how to make bread, his bread would be the best in the world. Angels may make mistakes, God might fool around and test his followers, but her son, even though he rebelled against his father, was still the best.

The mother's memory was confused. She called her eldest son Khalid Ahmed Zaki, killed two years before in the marshes of Iraq, by the younger one's name. Her soft lips trembled as she mentioned her eldest, Khalid. Enough. She did not want to hear or see. Her voice quavered. Again she called her living son Khalid, and then she grabbed the woman's arm.

"Stay with me. Let's have lunch together. I do have the right to cry. If you have a cat for a few months, you cry if it is lost. What about me? I watched my first son grow for thirty years and then he left, never to return. And here is my second one following him. Why do they do it? Why do they want to die?"

The woman's heart flooded with bitterness as her tongue searched for words to comfort the mother. What words can match such a delirium of anguish, such pain and loneliness? When would the mother stop blaming others? She walked slowly to the next room, avoiding the clutter, and returned with an old photo album. The house was stuffed with furniture but it was a cold house, empty of human warmth. There was abundant food, but it was tasteless. The old mother (why did she call her old? she was forty-five at most!) was using her hands to voice her anger, thrusting them into the air as if calling on somebody, then letting them fall in a gesture of pain. O mothers of a country that has long known naught but fear and oppression, how quickly old age descends upon your bodies and minds! Are they really asking for the world? They only wanted a day when they could talk freely without fear of persecution instead of whispering behind closed doors. Why must they be branded sinners, traitors, or other accusatory words as old as history itself?

"Will you come and see me again?"

"Yes."

"I suffer from rheumatism."

"I'll bring you medicine next time."

"Do you understand? Do you understand what they've done to us? The first one died, the second one left. My husband is crippled. The security men keep visiting me."

"What do they want?"

"Their questions are always the same: 'Has

anyone been in touch with you or visited you? Any news of your son? Don't be afraid. We won't tell on you.'"

"Do you have any other message for him?"

"Tell my son to keep warm and eat well, because he has a weak chest. Make him read his books and study. The exams are soon."

That was the last time I saw Um Khalid. After years of fighting and traveling from country to country, her son returned home, ill and exhausted. She was no longer there.

When, in the flush of youth, she applied to join the party, did she know what she would have to face? Things are always clearer from a distance. Killing and torture are only words, something that happened to somebody else. But when you reduce the distance, get close to people and start to recognize features, voices, gestures, and emotions, words take on a different meaning. Words are made into matter. So "kill" might mean "kill Nasier and Saïd"; "execute" might mean "execute Ali and Mustafa"; "torture," "torture Abbas and Mustafa." Words embody the execution of our history and our own demise. And once the distance has been reduced you can remember a person vividly, even after meeting him for only a few moments.

Years later, while living in Damascus, the woman was visited by a Lebanese friend who had fought with the Palestinians. While they were having dinner, the friend told her about a young man killed by the security forces. His body was found scattered all over the place. Before he died, he was tortured, dynamite was fastened to his body, and then he was tied under a bridge in Beirut and blown up. This image scared her. She stopped eating, then sighed, "It was to be expected, a very ordinary murder by a fascist regime." That was the end of the story for her. He was another person to be added to the list of the dead.

One evening five years later, visiting an old friend in West Germany, she escaped the family ritual of showing off the children and took refuge in a room full of books. Looking through some of them, she came across a booklet full of lists of people who had been killed, executed, or who had disappeared in Iraq during recent years. Some had their photos printed. There were many pages of names—list after list, arranged in columns according to the date of disappearance or execution. At first, she took in one name after the other, trying to identify them. Then the names began to resemble one another. She turned the pages and looked at the pictures. Under the first one, a mutilated body, a pile of wrinkled flesh, she read: "Abdul Jabar Abdullah, kidnapped in Beirut, was discovered after being blown up under a bridge. We condemn the murder by the agents of the fascist Iraqi regime in Lebanon." The voices of the children in the other room grew fainter. The adults' voices diminished. The sounds of the flute being played by her friend disappeared. Her eyes were huge sockets, her head a heavy bulk of steel and her legs soft old rags. She fell to the floor, her legs twisted beneath her. Her eyes looked further into the past, back to the years of fear and suspicion, to a young man in his twenties, a teacher who used to visit her at her workplace. With slow, heavy steps and a body that he seemed forced to carry, he would pull up a chair in front of her desk, lean on it, and sit down with a vacant look. Her mother saw him sitting like that. When he left, she said, "Poor man! He looks like a dove with a broken wing!"

Sometimes, considering her a font of information, he would ask her about their mutual friends. Avoiding his questions, she would respond ambiguously, "I don't know, I haven't seen him for a long time . . . probably . . . maybe." Thus their conversation ran, since both were treading a familiar level of mistrust. She could not forget his arrest and then release. In that country, only death could prove your innocence. Abdul Jabar was alive, so he was accused of betraying others. She wanted to know him better, to talk to him, and show her understanding. But only if she could be less afraid, less suspicious, because at that time he needed her friendship more than anything else. Now she recognized his picture, identifed what was left of the person she had known. He materialized before her. Tearfully, she remembered the time years before when she would meet him and listen to him. From the moment he arrived he would talk about music and literature. He used to play the flute and carry it with him wherever he went. Later somebody told her that after leaving Iraq for Beirut, more isolated than ever, he had gone mad. Mad . . . have we not all been accused of madness?

"Didn't I say you'd fall asleep?" said Saad sarcastically when she woke after her night watch at the base.

One step, two steps. The Kalashnikov* got heavier by the minute. It was dawn. Her body cried out for warmth. Her one desire was for a cup of tea and a warm bed, any bed. The night before, she could not sleep. Wrapped in a blanket on the floor, she had felt something crawl over her legs, arms, and hair. She thought it was her allergy to wool. The next morning, her face was covered in a red rash and her body itched furiously. She went down to the *rubar* and, behind the bushes, took down her trousers. Her legs were covered in the same rash. After making sure there was no one around, she washed her hair and body several times.

When Abu Samira saw her pouring herself some hot tea, he asked, "How are you?"

"I haven't slept all night. It must be my allergy to wool."

Falih laughed loudly when he heard her response and explained, "Don't accuse your poor allergy of the crime. The culprits are our old friends the bedbugs and head lice. They sensed

* A Russian-made machine gun widely used by fighters.

you were a newcomer and welcomed you in their inimitable way."

She promised herself that when she returned home she would sleep all night long under her cotton duvet. And she vowed to stop her habit of reading late into the night.

"Have you read *Revolution and Counter-Revolution?*" a comrade once asked her.

"No."

Embarrassed by her ignorance, she had rushed to the nearest bookshop and spent all night reading.

"Have you read *Literature and Revolution?*"

"No."

Walk fast, she had told herself. It is better not to wait for the bus. The bookshop might be closed if the bus is late.

"Your shift is over, you can sleep now."

She had four hours sleep. When she got up, the base was almost deserted. Falih was about to leave to gather wood. For a moment she remembered her mother. Remembered her getting up every morning, ready to tidy the house the minute they left. At those times her mother looked absentminded. She would pick up cups and plates automatically, clear the table and start washing up. She did the same thing for over twenty years, like a robot. She remembered her mother whispering, talking to herself: "What are we going to cook today?" Nobody would answer. The memory frightened her. She imagined a blindfolded person going round in the same circle, day after day, year after year. She was ten years old when her father bought their first gas cooker. So as to avoid learning how to cook, she stood beside her mother and pretended to be afraid that the cooker might explode. Her mother spent hours trying to teach her how to use it. In the end, she gave up.

Now she told Abu Samira that she was an expert at gathering wood, offering to help Falih. Abu Samira said there was nothing about her to indicate she possessed such a skill, but to avoid the same argument they had the day before, he assented.

Why did Falih look so upset? His face was dark and tense, and he looked as though he was having trouble breathing. His steps were quick, his body stiff. On that sunny, cold day, he looked at her with the suppressed anger of someone obliged to do something unwillingly. Falih would be killed three years later in an attack on an army platoon.

She wrapped the *yashmag*\* around her head, covering her nose and mouth. She looked like a little boy. On the path the shepherds used on their way to the top of the mountain, Falih stopped and pointed to the trunk of a dead tree. "Let's chop it into pieces. The rest of the group will be along shortly to collect it." Having climbed fast, she could feel warmth spreading through her body. In the distance she saw a lonely shepherd gazing up at a sky as blue and clear as crystal. Are not the stars tempted to glow in daytime on a day like this?

She said, "I'll gather wood on the other side." Falih nodded in agreement as he struggled with the trunk. He seemed so lonely, speaking his private language, seeking not to communicate, but to pursue a long, desperate monologue with himself. Should she follow the shepherd, she wondered, or follow the mountain goats in their slow search for grazing? Should she make for the summit, with its lonely tree? She felt a wave of joy that prompted her to climb higher. Her steps became lighter as she walked by herself, no longer having to gaze at

\* A checkered headscarf.

the back of the person ahead of her. She was alone. She did not have to conform to another's way of thinking or behaving. Alone, she felt no need to pacify others. Alone, she had no need to excel or compete. She felt close to the cold clods of earth, close to the stones she kicked down the valley, close to the grass and sky. She felt brave enough to demand the stars should shimmer by day. And she saw in this moment of euphoria the *Beshmarga*\* descending the mountain. They looked at her; she returned their looks and continued climbing. She forgot the wood, Falih, and his dead trunk. It was as if she had gained the ability to fly. She moved like a wild horse that had forgotten its breaking and regained its freedom as it galloped in the fields. She climbed and climbed the bare mountain, its grass eaten by the large numbers of mountain goats. She, too, was climbing a mountain unruined by humans. What time was it? Darkness started to compete with the blue sky. Gray lines invaded it, grays that seemed to reflect the summit rose in the sky. Or was it the other way around? Was the mountain with its few inhabitants, its herds and plants, a reflection of the sky and its various

\* Kurdish fighters.

— 73 —

colors? She turned around but could not see a soul. In front of her, she saw a dry cave. There was nothing but silence, early darkness, and fresh air. Where was Falih? How was she going to get back? Where were her wings? Where was the crystal blue sky, where was the end of the journey?

She sat on a rock at the entrance to the cave, well wrapped in her coat, soothing herself. Yes, they would soon start looking for her. If she were in her city, she would need no one to show her the way. She would not be lost. She knew its streets and roads; she knew all its plazas and bridges without need of a map. She would walk from house to house, street to street, full of love for that city.

You, sitting on a rock at the mouth of a cave, wrapped in the coat of a fleeing soldier, where will your foolishness end? Ah, the sound of a shot in the distance . . . and another shot, nearer. She got up from her rock. Maybe it would have been better if she had stayed in the same place. Another shot, much closer. She could not wait. Running, she descended, followed by little stones. Then she started to slow down . . . slower . . . slower . . .

# BIG BROTHER

I'll tell on you if you don't stop doing that. Stop it! Or I'll tell mother!"

The more she ignored him, the louder he became. He was screaming now, as if to prove that he was really bigger and stronger.

"I said stay where you are! Stop running! Aren't you afraid I will tell Mother? Fine, I will tell Father then!" She ran ahead of him, ignoring his shouts, threats, and frantic gesticulations. She did not even notice him waving her towards the house. She was skipping, laughing, and chattering to imaginary children running alongside her. She was always leaping and gliding on tiptoes to a tune only she could hear, like a ballerina getting ready for a solo performance. "Stop doing that! Don't put your bag on your head! Carry it in your hand!"

It annoyed him to no end that she liked to put her box-shaped school bag on her head and sway left and right as she ran along. What horrid behavior! How would he, her big brother, take care of her, look after her safety, protect her? How could he keep her from harm every day as they went to school from home and back? He hated having her around. It meant that he could not play with his friends. He hated his mother's insistent nagging:

"Hold her hand! Don't let her walk alone! Don't let her cross the street by herself! Make sure she behaves properly in the street! Don't let her go to class with chewing gum in her mouth!"

He grew tired of chasing after her, yelling at her, and trying to hold her hand against her will. He let go one day after he had forced open her mouth to make sure there was no chewing gum inside. He walked ahead of her calmly, trying to look like a mature young man at the age of eight. He left her behind to skip and run as she liked. He pretended to ignore her. But before long he began to worry, especially when he could not hear the pencils, pencil sharpener, and colorful beads rattling in her bag, when he could not hear her fluttering all over the place, and when no squealing could be heard behind him as she ran into things. He wanted to turn around and make sure she was all right, but he stopped himself. He slowed his pace and hoped that she would catch up with him, but he did not turn around to check on her or wait for her. He was afraid she would laugh at him for not sticking to his threats.

He reached home first. He found the door slightly ajar but the curtains drawn. He pushed his way in and walked to the kitchen as usual, calling out, "Mama, I'm hungry." His mother kissed him and told him to wait a while. It was a hot day and he could see signs of fatigue on her face. She looked big in the kitchen. He watched her sit down on a stool, spreading her legs slightly to give her pregnant belly a comfortable space to settle into.

"Where is your sister?" His heart raced at the reminder of her. He pretended he did not hear his mother, looking intently at the pots and pans piled neatly against one wall. He heard his mother again, this time her voice loud and urgent. "Where is your little sister?"

He turned away, wanting to disappear from the face of the earth. Then he exploded, tears glistening in his eyes, "I told you a thousand times she never listens to me! I told her to walk beside me, hold my hand, carry her bag like all other girls, but she wouldn't. She laughed at me! I smacked her but she stuck out her tongue at me and crossed the street all by herself, just to annoy me! I don't know where she is."

His mother didn't wait any longer. She shot up from her stool, too quickly for someone with her large belly. She looked everywhere in the house, in the courtyard and the three rooms. Maybe her daughter was hiding in a corner playing with her toys and speaking to herself, as she often did. She grabbed her abaya, jerked it off the coat hanger next to the door, thrust the curtain to one side, and ran into the street that led to her daughter's school. "Stupid boy! How many times did I tell you to watch over her? She is only five; it is your responsibility to look after your little sister! Oh God, keep her safe this time. Let me find her in one piece!" She ran, imagining scene after scene of horrible accidents, each ending with her daughter covered in blood. Did she drown in a nearby ditch? Did a car hit her? She ran, tripping on her abaya now and letting it slip down her head again. She ran with a tightened chest and quickened breath. She felt a new kind of pain close in on her heart, which was now a bundle of fear and worry. "Why did he leave her behind, stupid boy? Why did he not watch over her as I told him, why did God have to punish me with such a weak boy?"

She turned right onto the alley leading to the heart of the Suq.* She hated going through the Suq, and had taught her boy to avoid it despite the

---

* The market in any Arab or Muslim city.

and kissed it. She loved him so much, much more than her mother. He played with her and tickled her. He laughed more than her busy, glum mother. She saw him for only a short while every evening after he came home from work and before he went to see his friends at the café. But he teased her, hugged her, and protected her from her mother's anger and her brother's sharp looks. He always found excuses for her and beat her big brother instead.

Her brother was locked in the cupboard under the stairs. He was being punished for his negligence. He curled up in a dark corner and heard nothing but his sister's sobs and hiccups. He felt an overwhelming rage, an endless tidal wave drowning his fear and throwing up anger and resentment. "I don't want to be anybody's brother. I don't want to be responsible for anyone. I don't want to be her brother." He spewed out the last sentence violently, wanting the words to envelop her like a cloud so dark, an abaya so black that she would never be able to find escape from it. Not even her hands would be seen again. He wanted to break her schoolbag. He wanted to twist her mouth so hard that she would forget how to laugh.

He wanted to crush her legs into so many pieces that she would never jump again, not in front of him, not behind him. He wished he would grow up quickly. He would beat her again and again, until she fell to the ground, until she grabbed his hand, kissed it, and begged him, "I'm sorry, forgive me."

# ANOTHER SHORE

Like a child, my mother hated darkness. She would switch on all the lights in the house to make sure everyone was all right.

One day, she told me, "When I die, put lights around my grave."

That little woman with big black eyes, full lips, and a round face, that woman who hated walking the streets alone, hated shopping alone, hated sleeping in the dark, went to the Ministry of Defense alone for weeks on end. At the rear gate there was an information office dealing with political detainees. My mother had one preoccupation: to leave home early each morning with a cardboard box containing a towel, some clothes, and tins of food. To the officer in charge, the sergeant and soldiers, she would repeat the same sentences: "Take the box. My daughter needs clothes. She was not allowed to take anything with her when she was arrested."

The answers were likewise the same: "We haven't got a prisoner here by that name. Who said we have political prisoners here? Don't you know we are living through a new era, the era of the Progressive National Front?"

A strange silence permeated the house, its

rooms, and the garden. In the street outside, the silence was different. The neighbors said nothing as they tried to avoid watching my mother carry her cardboard box to and from a place they knew only too well. They avoided looking and listening so they would not be accused of sympathizing with her. They would casually close their garden gates and doors and pull down their blinds. The few yards separating our house from theirs became miles dense with suspicion and isolation. In time, the neighbors stopped visiting our house altogether.

Eventually, my mother no longer questioned the officer. She began taking her youngest daughter along with her and the two of them sat in front of the ministry's gate. Sweating in the baking sun of August, covered in her abaya, her daughter bored and complaining of a persistent headache, my mother was seen by every person who went into the ministry, morning and afternoon. Her constant presence provoked whispers and enquiries. Many people avoided looking at her, at her box. One day, a soldier approached and asked, "*Khala,** why are you sitting here?"

* "Aunt" in Arabic.

Before she had time to answer, the sergeant shouted at the soldier to leave her be, not to interfere. On the tenth day, the officer ordered the sergeant to get rid of her. He managed to move her away from the gate. The next morning, my mother and her daughter, my sister, took their place a few yards away. At the end of the third week, the sergeant called her, saying:

"What's your daughter's name? Give me the box. Go home."

She gazed in awe at the cruel face with its thick mustache, handed over the box, and began to cry. At home, a smile lighting up her face, she forbore my father's anger and bitterness. "Didn't I tell you? She's still alive!"

# VISITATION

We sat around the sole paraffin heater—circle after circle of women forced to live together. Circle after circle of flaccid bodies and wrinkled skin. Circle after circle of unbearable silence. Our features were empty, our eyes focused on nothing. Sometimes I would see others lying awake at night as if hanging on to the days gone by. Farewell, past life. Farewell, children. Farewell, home. Farewell to the pain of a sadness that tore my heart apart.

"Good morning. You have visitors," Um Wahid shouted in her piercing voice. She did not walk, she ran, waving her arm while trying at the same time to fix her black head cover with a golden pin.

"Dr. Fatima Al-Khurasani gave me this pin. After her arrest, they brought her to this very cell and she chose me out of all the prisoners to serve her," Um Wahid said proudly. "Dr. Fatima belonged to the Baha'i sect and was imprisoned four years. A few months after her release, she was killed. They said her young lover killed her. They said the same regime that had imprisoned her killed her."

When Um Wahid had heard of Dr. Fatima's murder, she went into shock and began slapping her own face and breasts. Then she asked Al-Alwaya, the guard, to fetch her a quarter kilogram of *halawa tamir*.* That evening, all the prisoners gathered in the yard and read *Al-Fatiha*,** crying bitterly and hiding their faces with their *foota*.*** Some of them slapped chests as hard as they could, while Al-Alwaya led them in reciting words and mourning. Um Wahid offered *halawa tamir* and they commiserated with her.

"You have a visitor." That was Um Jassim's voice. Why did I remain seated, shivering? I went along the concrete corridor to the yard and then to another building where the governess's, secretary's, and guard's rooms were. Outside was another yard, empty except for four concrete benches and four guards, two of whom were women. My mother was seated on one of the benches, and my father paced back and forth in the yard. During the visit, the questions we could not utter haunted us. I wanted to ask about my friends. They wanted to know what had happened to me. Instead, for half an hour, we exchanged banalities.

* A kind of dessert made of dates, served at a funeral.
** The first chapter of the *Qur'an*. In some Muslim societies, *Al-Fatiha* is read by people who gather to remember the dead.
*** A headscarf, part of traditional Iraqi dress.

"Are you all right?"

"Yes."

"Do you sleep well?"

"Yes, I am all right and sleep well."

"Is the food edible?"

"Yes."

"Do you need money?"

"No, thank you."

We sat there, the three of us, trading banalities as if we had lost our common language. I asked about my grandmother, aunt, and brothers. They asked me how I spent my time. Between each question, they exchanged worried looks. The visit came to an end. Why do words of departure have the sting of salt water? My mother hugged me and whispered in a quavering voice, "Have they treated you badly?"

"No, everything is all right."

She looked suspiciously at my face covered in inflamed sores. I was alarmed by her calm sadness, her wet eyes, her silence. They were much harder to bear than crying would have been. My heart was bursting.

"One of the neighbors told me she saw you

taken by car to the forensic medicine depart-
ment."

"No, I was never there."

They left me with tired steps, as if old age had
suddenly caught up with them.

# BACK TO
# NAWCHILICAN

In a small village, in a small house at the foot of a green mountain, in a hut on the edge of a spring, in a room that functioned as a library, there lived for many years a group of dreaming fighters, traitors, and a few killers. Most of them are now dead. Their names are unforgettable: Abu Samira, Abu Jaffar, his wife and children, Falih, Jassim, Qadir, Fakhri, Farouq, Sabir, Mudhafar, Faïez, Sabri, Hazim, Omar, and Abu Layla. The prism of time refracts the light into thousands of rays. I stand with my hands open and embrace them. I see these people clearly. How many are alive to see me?

QASR AL-NIHAYA

They are waiting for you," Al-Alwaya, the female guard said.

The place was unusually silent. The prisoners did not wave good-bye because they did not guess what was going to happen to me. If the authorities were going to release me, as they said they would, why did they send three armed men to accompany me? My whole body was wracked with pain as sound filled my head. What is happening? Where are they taking me? Have they arrested more comrades? Why do I have to see the same ugly faces? I wished I could stay with the prisoners instead of going with the three men. This was my second trip with them. Why?

"Hello. How are you?"

"Fine, thank you."

I walked between two of them. The third trailed behind. In the car they kept asking questions about my health, as if it was the thing they cared most about in the world. They laughed loudly and traded jokes and talked about the beauty of living in freedom, about prison life and short visits. One of them spoke with concern about my studies. Was I going back to college to continue them?

"Did you know that the three people arrested a few days before you were executed?"

"Yes."

Anyone overhearing us would think we were one big, happy family, exchanging news about relatives and friends.

"Have you received any letters or heard any news since you've been in prison?"

"No."

"Why do you lie? We know you've received messages."

"I've received nothing."

"Then you must have sent messages to warn the others."

"No. I haven't sent anything."

My body begins to tremble. My mind loses its grip on nerves and muscles. Fear grows like a weed. The world shrinks. The sun shines but I cannot see it. The day passes slowly by but I do not feel a thing. Here is the Qasr again. Here is the corridor, the room, the doorway. I close the door behind me. I wake up tired, exhausted by the short or long trip I have taken. I am sweating, my skin oozes salty water. My skin cries, my fingers tremble, and I stare for hours at the tip of my white shoe. Something has died inside me. No, it was not my heavy heart, or the fear. It was a pain deep down in my uterus that spread quickly into my whole abdomen. A long, silent, dead conversation. I wished I could cover my head and body with a blanket and escape to a place where no torturer could enquire about my health or my studies.

It was evening. I heard footsteps on the marble floor and the door handle turn. I saw a fat face precariously balanced on a fat body. I followed a beckoning hand into the corridor and then turned left into a room with a huge desk in it. Was this to be the stage set for a rerun of the old play? Bulging eyes hid behind dark glasses. The suit was elegant. The beads of the rosary clicked gently. I stood there in silence for long minutes.

"It has come to our attention that while you were in prison, you were still in touch with certain bastards and that you, bitch, sent them information about what was happening to you. Don't you realize we know everything? Do you think you are anything other than a whore? Don't you know how strong we are? Do you think a few whores and bastards can jeopardize our government?"

Yes, here I was in the middle of act one. On stage. Here was the interrogator and there were the torturers, standing off to one side, bored. I was face to face with a pair of blazing eyes. Why the anger? That was the new element in this exceedingly long play. When was this black comedy going to end?

"Do you think that *zita** like you can change anything?"

"No."

"Give her a pen and paper. Come here and write:

I, the undersigned, joined the Communist Party on . . . and was arrested on . . . In my room were found hand grenades, explosives, and pamphlets against the revolutionary government and the Progressive National Front. I state of my own free will that I did not join the party for political reasons, but to meet men and have sex with as many of

---

* Very small birds found in the marshes of southern Iraq. To refer to someone as zita is an insult.

them as I could. My relationships were all immoral. I admit I had sex with . . . and I affirm that I was not a virgin when I entered Qasr al-Nihaya. I have been well treated by the security forces.

Sign and date your confession.

"Come here. Read what you have written into the tape recorder clearly and loudly."

"Yes. I the undersigned joined the Communist Party on . . . and was arrested on . . ."

I read into the microphone. I was taken from this office to another one. Mugshots were taken. Forms were signed. Yes, all right.

Throughout my childhood I wore a special necklace. My grandmother insisted I wear it. It was made of brightly colored material and inside it were folded pieces of paper. One day, with the encouragement of my older brother, I decided to take a closer look at the mysterious bits of paper. Hiding in the dark under the stairs, trembling with fear and excitement, we both unfolded the charms. We could not read what was written on them. There were symbols, but no words, or unfamiliar words at best.

My grandmother was a great believer in magic, and in the blind palm reader who lived on the other side of town. She liked to make a to-do about hiring a taxi to cross the bridge to go to the blind woman's house. She complained she had to wait a long time for my sake. My grandmother said, "The blind palm reader told me this child must wear charms around her neck for ten years. These will protect her from evil." The palm reader had predicted my life would be far from easy.

Here I am, years later, writing, repeating things long after the blind palm reader, my grandmother, my mother, and many of my friends and comrades have died. Is it my way of ridding my body of the sickness that wracked it the day I was touched by those I hated so? Is it my way of warding off forgiveness that comes with time? Warding off failing memory or returning to a country where they still practice such repulsive rituals? Warding off memory's conscious emptying of its rage? Warding off oblivion, oblivion.

# HEART, WHAT HAVE
# YOU SEEN?

Abu Ghraib, August 20

Pointing to the last cell at the end of the corridor, the guard said in a loud voice, "There is barely any room left for more prisoners. You must stay with Um Wahid, Um Jassim, and Um Ali."

Slowly I followed the big woman's steps. She was in her forties. Her hair was jet black and her body a huge mass of fat that vibrated with every step: left, right, buttock up, leg down, left, right. I did not know what to do with my right hand. I kept trying to adjust the strap of my handbag, but then realized I was not even carrying one. I put my hands in the pockets of my navy blue skirt, took them out, put them back in. Slowly, I followed the guard's steps. She was wearing a gray uniform. The walls, floor, and ceiling were concrete. Were the women made of the same substance?

The front of each cell was made of iron bars with a door on the right-hand side. There were two rows of cells with iron bars facing each other. The corridor was a yard wide. To maintain some privacy, the women knotted old, gray blankets to the bars to serve as bizarre makeshift curtains.

Many eyes stared at me, the eyes of women with their bodies wrapped in black clothes. The whole place was black and gray, like an old family photo. The women's faces were a strange color. Not pale in the usual way, but they held the pallor of illness and fatigue. In their faces I beheld the dryness and cracking of earth that has suffered drought for many years. The concrete floor did not nourish seeds, the light bulbs surrounded by wire did not give light.

The guard stopped at the last cell and told the three women behind bars, "This is the new prisoner. She's a political."

She pronounced the word slowly and firmly, as if introducing a new breed of animal. Then she left.

I did not know what to do so I stood where I was, hoping one of them would make the first move. The cell was a square-shaped cube with two small, curtained windows with bars, looking out onto another concrete wall a few yards away. In the right-hand corner there was a cubicle big enough to accommodate one person sitting or standing. It was the toilet and the bathroom, the place where the three women could wash their dishes, their clothes, and their bodies. In it was a tap and a pitcher used to clean one's body after using the toilet. The two walls of the cubicle were so low they barely covered the lower part of one's body. The entrance was decorated with an old cotton nightdress.

For years, the women had been cutting up old blankets and clothes for use as curtains. They hung them up in the afternoon when the prison governess left, and took them down in the morning before she arrived for inspection. With endless determination, they persisted in the same ritual, as if proving to themselves and the others that, in enjoying some privacy, they could still defy the system.

It was evening. One woman, the smallest one, had long braids and wore a black, long-sleeved dress over striped pajamas. She carried her mattress on her head and walked out of the cell, staggering under the heavy load. The second woman did the same. She was very old and wrinkled, with gums that made unusual sounds. Her face was covered in tattoos. The blue tattoos began at her eyebrows and continued to her navel, as she later proudly showed us. Was she in her eighties? She carried her mattress on her head and left. The third woman stood next to me.

"Do you have a mattress?"

"No."

"Have you any clothes apart from what you're wearing?"

"No."

She peered at my face, particularly at my chin covered in sores. Then she put her mattress on her head and told me to follow her.

"My name is Um Wahid. The little woman is Um Jassim. She's sentenced to fifteen years. Old Um Ali will be released in two years. The governess lets us sleep in the yard because it's impossible to sleep inside in this heat."

I sat down on the mattress Um Wahid had lent me. Um Wahid was the longest serving prisoner in the women's prison. She had been sentenced to life, along with her brother. They had murdered her husband. Shortly after their wedding, her husband had treated her badly, beating her up and forcing her to entertain his friends. One morning while her husband was at work, she had packed her bags and left, returning to her family in Al-'Amara, in the South. Her mother had sent her back straightaway, saying, "Your home now is with your husband. We don't want you anymore."

Um Wahid told her young brother that her husband was forcing her to be a prostitute. Together they agreed the only solution was to kill him. So they did. At the time she was nineteen and her brother was seventeen.

Over the years, Um Wahid had accumulated many aluminum plates, pans, spoons, pillows, clothes, and blankets. Being there for such a long time, she was the official recipient of the prisoners' leftovers, the things they did not want to take with them upon release, their reminders of prison.

My bed was next to Um Jassim's in the concrete yard surrounded by a high barbed wire fence. My continual coughing drove someone to complain. I heard one of them say, "Maybe she's suffering from TB."

At that moment, for no good reason (maybe it was the sympathy shown by Um Wahid, or the other women's silence, or the complaints some of them made), the mask I had worn for weeks began to crack. The mask had protected me from seeing, smelling, touching, but not from hearing—hearing the voices of the tortured, trying to recognize their identities, hearing the torturers' footfalls in the corridors of the Qasr, listening to the sound of keys turning in locks, trying to identify the last click before the torturer would appear before me. I touched my disheveled hair, matted with dirt and dried blood. I smelled the odor of my body, emitted most strongly from between my blood-smeared legs. I touched my hair, my face, and I cried. I cried quietly, a painful, continuous moaning that lasted all night, during which I mourned my disappointments, my fear, and the longing I had to see my friends and comrades.

Can the soul be separated from its shell and leave it behind to wander the open fields? I gaze into the darkness. I see a green mountain, heavy with bushes and cypress trees. At its foot are vineyards, overlooking a village. The tinkling of water can be heard inside the houses. I see a group of children picking up chamomile leaves, putting them in cotton bags, competing with each other to fill them up. I see them eating figs on their way home and throwing walnuts at each other. I see myself laughing happily with them.

August 21

At last it is morning. We carry our mattresses and blankets on our heads as we form a unique black and gray parade marching to our cells. One, two. One, two. Good morning, cell! Here are four women to crowd you, together with their clothes in cardboard boxes, their aluminum plates. Good morning, cell! Good morning, toilet! The place four women call home. Good morning, old clothes, shredded to be used for periods, washed and hung to dry on a line that only appears at night! Good morning, my home for the next six months, the smell of which is a mixture of toilet, period cloths hung to dry, and pieces of wet *husain** on the floor, kept damp to cool down the heat reflected from the concrete floor, walls, and ceiling! Good morning, withered bodies in long sleeves and black head coverings protecting us from the long years of drought!

Um Wahid said, "You're lucky to be put in with us. We lifers are the best women here. You're lucky they didn't put you in with the women over there." With this, she pointed to the wing opposite ours, separated from us by a sandy yard. She meant the prostitutes' wing.

* Agricultural packaging material such as potato or rice sacks.

Um Jassim threw her mattress onto the floor, and despite the unbearable heat, covered her head with a blanket and slept. I followed Um Ali and Um Wahid, the latter carrying a teapot, and joined the queue of women waiting for bread and tea before a small opening in the kitchen wall. I did not understand the necessity for hurrying, but Um Ali, chewing over her words with her gums and tongue, explained that as the beverage disappeared from the huge can, the cook would add more water, so that if you were late, you would get only a pot of thin yellowish liquid that bore little resemblance to tea.

Nothing aroused more curiosity than the arrival of a new prisoner. For days, we questioned each other. Among the answers I received, Um Wahid expressed her happiness at the death of her husband, claiming at the same time that she was innocent. She was happy in prison, a feeling that diminished only when her mother came to visit. After each visit, Um Wahid would cover her head and cry quietly in her corner.

"My mother comes just to find out the date of my release. I know her. I know what she's planning for me and my brother. She hasn't forgiven me for what I did to my brother, life imprisonment for her son. Yes, I know what she's planning for me, so I've begged the governess to keep my release date a secret. The problem is I'll be released the same day as my brother. I've begged the governess to delay my release for a few days or, even better, to grant it a few days earlier. My mother will send her brother to fetch us. I know how she loathes me. I know that, whenever she looks at me, she's accusing me of wasting her son's life. I know, too, what she's planning for us both. My brother's life will be in danger after his release, because my murdered husband's family will avenge his death. It can only be avenged if they kill one of my family. The way my mother looks at me, her interest in my release makes me realize she's promised the dead man's family my life. She can spare them the act of vengeance, and the punishment that would follow, if my uncle kills me on the day of my release. He will get the protection of the law. Six months is all he'll get for protecting the family's honor. That's why I have to pretend to agree with her all the time."

Each woman had her own lullaby, her own nighttime song. Um Jassim was different. She had a dreamy look and walk that separated her from the rest. Owing to her mental illness, she was exempt from cleaning the corridors and helping in the kitchen, and was allowed to stay in bed late. Her daily routine was simple: she lay in bed until eleven a.m., completely covered, no matter how hot it was, by her gray blanket. She would have lunch with us and then go back to bed. Sometimes she would make the effort and attend the literacy class, but more often than not she stayed in her cell, talking to her husband.

In the evening, after Um Jassim and Um Ali left for the yard with their mattresses on their heads, Um Wahid would help me take a bath. She would put a plank of wood over the toilet basin for me to stand on, then fill a bucket with water. My long hair was the main problem. It was matted with dirt and blood. I could not get it clean. Um Wahid went to the guard to ask for a pair of scissors. To be on the safe side, the guard supervised the operation.

"Dogs . . . sons of bitches!" Um Wahid murmured as she cut my hair. The guard looked sharply at her, took the scissors and left. Um Wahid said: "She isn't living any better than us. Her salary is very low. She works six days a week and her son is a soldier fighting in Kurdistan. She's a prisoner like we are."

August 22

The prison governess ordered us back to our cells because one of the prisoners had attacked a guard. The heat was unbearable; Um Jassim was delirious, calling out to her husband loudly. Um Wahid dampened her pillow with water and slept. Um Ali was snoring. At midnight, a noise shattered the quasi-silence of the wing. It came from Najma's cell. She was the cook, and the only prisoner who persisted in wearing heavy makeup. More noise. I got up and whispered:

"Um Jassim. Um Jassim."

I told her about the noise. She smiled calmly, "Don't worry, it's the guard. She's pulling up her bed to sleep next to Najma. Go to sleep, don't worry."

September 2

My parents visited me once a week. It was a torment for us all. The prison is located at the edge of the city, so my father drove for hours to get here and back. They both seemed very ill.

Since they had already been sentenced, the other prisoners were allowed visits once a month. Um Jassim's health deteriorated, and she was swallowing large doses of tranquillizers. She spent most of her time facing the wall, wrapped in her blanket, lost in a dreamy state. We were there next to her, but she saw nothing but the past. Like children taking in a horror film, we sat there mesmerized, watching her wither. We had to stay together in the cell, waiting for the arrival of night so we could sleep away our boredom and fear. Night then witnessed our longing for daylight, when we might recover our sanity, our release from persistent insomnia, and the sounds of women moaning.

Over the last few weeks, I watched women fighting over nothing, pulling each other's hair, banging their heads against the walls, and laughing hysterically. We watched and listened as Um Jassim addressed her dead husband, saying: "When will it be my turn to be with you? Why, why? Haven't I loved you more than anything else in the world? Haven't I waited for you every night, to look after you!" Um Jassim continued this in her monotonous voice, asking the question again and again. Um Wahid could take it no longer and began shouting, "Enough! Enough!"

She tore her dress, ripping it from the neckline, and beat herself. It took Um Ali and me a quarter of an hour to calm her down. Meanwhile Um Jassim was still reciting, "Why, why?"

October 1
The slow awakening, the slow morning, the slow shuffle to the kitchen to get tea. I heard the other women whispering. There must be a newcomer! Um Wahid turned her head aside to avoid looking at the newcomer and said, "As if prostitution wasn't enough, she's pregnant."

Realizing what the others thought and felt about her, the black woman in the red dress stood at the end of the queue, carrying her small teapot, waiting patiently for the yellowish brew.

In the afternoon, seeing us sitting on the concrete steps, she walked hesitantly towards us and sat at a distance. I went and sat next to her and asked her name.

"Since early childhood they've called me Al-Abda, the Black. I've accepted it to the extent that I've forgotten my real name." The other inmates didn't like her behavior. How dare she come to their wing and try to talk to them? She was not one of them. They looked at her so aggressively that the poor woman had to walk away as fast as she could.

For the tenth time, Um Wahid asked me to read Mudhafar Al-Nawab's poem *The Rail and Hamad* to her. Again she cried.

October 6

One morning Um Jassim surprised us. She did not say good morning to the wall, but turned around and said it to us. Um Wahid thought we should celebrate the occasion. We collected two hundred and fifty *fils*, gave it to Um Wahid, and she made a beeline for Al-Alwiya, the guard. In addition to her official tasks, Al-Alwiya sold us the few things we might need urgently. Explaining the reason for the celebration, Um Wahid asked her for four eggs. Um Wahid took the eggs to the kitchen and begged Najma to allow her to fry them. She consented, and Um Wahid promised Najma a new lipstick. Um Wahid was frantic with joy.

But we could not celebrate. The four eggs were bad. Um Wahid attacked Al-Alwiya when she refused to give us our money back. She was punished. She had to clean the corridor twice a day for two weeks.

Where was Al-Abda? We suddenly missed her silent presence, her red dress and huge belly. The guard ran to search the prostitutes' wing while we looked for her in the kitchen and elsewhere. Moments later, we heard Um Wahid's anxious voice calling us. We found her by the rubbish. Al-Abda was leaning against one of the dustbins. Her legs were bent, her red dress rolled up. Between her legs was a baby! With the sharp knife she always carried in her pocket the guard cut the umbilical cord, lifted the baby up, and smacked its bottom. After an hour, Al-Abda was taken to the hospital. Two days later, she returned alone.


November 11
Um Ali asked me to compose a petition requesting a special pardon due to her age. When I asked her age, she said, "Work it out for yourself. I was born the day my father came back from the war. That day, my mother had an accident. She slipped on the ground while carrying some wood. She twisted her ankle. I was born two hours later."

Um Ali was serving a life sentence. With her son she had killed her husband's assassin. She had immersed her hands in his blood and wandered along the dusty roads of her village, her hands held high, chanting how sweet was the taste of vengeance, how proud she was to defend the honor of her family.

We were all suffering from a bad attack of the flu, except for Um Jassim. She thought that the best prevention for flu was an onion, not to be eaten but worn about the neck like a necklace. She walked around now with a big onion dangling from her neck, adding a terrible new smell to the cell.

November 13
The only non-Iraqi prisoner among us was an Egyptian called Amira. Tall, talkative, she was an intimate friend of the governess. She was sentenced to five years for drug trafficking, along with a man she insisted was her fiancé. They were both innocent, she said, and did not know what they were carrying until the moment they were arrested. Her fiancé was executed a few months after the trial. She was iso-

lated. Nobody talked to her except Um Jassim, me, and Najma. She was in urgent need of money so she sold her fiancé's watch. I bought it: it was an Omega.

November 14

For the first time, Um Jassim was in the mood to talk to someone. Her words were incoherent, falling from her mouth like autumn leaves. Talk, talk. She held my hand as if afraid I would leave her alone with her past, her lacerated memories. What a foolish band we were!

"I still love him. He is my only love. I have five children. Have you heard me talking about them? He is my man. How jealous I felt! I will feel jealous until the day I die. Five years after our marriage, he began coming home late. He said he was only working longer hours for the children's and my sake. I was in charge of everything—the house, the children—and like a rabbit I had given him five children in five years. One day my cousin came to see me. He asked me how I felt about Mohammed's new wife! I can't describe how I felt at that moment. I can't remember whether I fed the children, bathed them, or just put them to bed.

All I could think of was Mohammed naked next to another woman. I had loved him long before our marriage. That night he came back drunk. I embraced him in a way I hadn't done for a long time. Why? Why? He made love to me and fell asleep straight afterwards. As if in a trance, I got up, took his gun, and shot him in the head, not once but four times. I can't remember what happened after that, but I've been told I dragged the naked body off the bed, lifted the drain cover in the yard, and pushed him down. Apparently, the children were around me at the time and saw what I did with their father. Still in my nightdress, covered in blood, I ran, followed by my children, to the police station where he worked as a policeman. For two years, they kept me in a mental hospital, force-fed me, and gave me electric shocks. This is my third year in this prison."

November 20

The guard read us an order:

"We will be visited by a group of friends from one of the socialist countries. They are coming to view our progress in the field of women's prison management. Tidy up the place, polish the bars and the kitchen, and wear your best clothes. Leave off your uniforms."

That order was followed in the evening by a surprise search of our wing by two guards from the men's prison. The result was the confiscation of three knives, two pairs of scissors, a china teapot, my poetry book *The Rail and Hamad*, and Najma's perfume and makeup.

After their departure women screamed, cried, and suffered fits. It was group hysteria, and it expressed their years of deprived freedom. Najma cried bitterly, her kohl smeared all over her face. Some of them banged their heads on the walls. Um Ali behaved as if she were still walking on the roads of her village, proud of her vengeance. She sang and danced and even recited poetry. We carried on through the night.

The day of the visit, the governess summoned me to her office and told me I would be kept out of sight until the visitors' departure. After all, we were living through the era of the National Front, an era of unity, freedom, and socialism, an era of no political prisoners!

The visit was a success, I was told. The prisoners all wore their best clothes and were on their best behavior, praising the government and the president for their kindness. Um Ali had shouted, "Long live the national government! Long live our guardian, the president!"

December 11

It was Friday afternoon. We were sitting on the concrete steps, enjoying the warm sun on a winter day. Um Athaba, a Bedouin with the most beautiful green eyes, was knitting a jumper for her daughter, who was being kept in an orphanage until her mother's release. Um Athaba was the last woman in Iraq to be sentenced to death by hanging. She was kept in the death cell for one year, but the law was changed meanwhile and capital punishment for women was abolished. Um Jassim was showing me the way she wrote the alphabet, and I was correcting her mistakes. I asked her to write it again. Um Wahid watched Najma try a new shade of lipstick a guard had just given her. The rest of the women were quiet, enjoying the calm of the afternoon. Suddenly, we heard a scream. It came from Um Ali, who was sitting near the other wing. She was holding a mirror borrowed from the guard. We ignored her. We were too relaxed to disturb ourselves for yet another manifestation of frustration and boredom. But her screams persisted for longer than usual and we got up. Um Ali stopped screaming and froze in a position that surprised us all. Her mouth was open wide, and with her finger she pointed inside. We pushed each other trying to look, but the guard won the privilege of looking first. Her face went pale and her teeth chattered.

"Allah Akbar . . . Allah Akbar," she moaned.

Um Ali was teething. According to one of the inmates, that meant only one thing: Um Ali was over a hundred years old!

December 15

Um Ali's petition was refused, despite the well-known fact of her teething. Um Athaba attacked Amira, the Egyptian, fracturing her skull with a brick. I jumped on Um Athaba, trying to stop her from killing Amira. Amira was taken to the hospital in the men's prison, the nearest one to us. I was called as a witness, while Um Athaba was transferred to solitary confinement pending her trial. I saw her after her interrogation, before she was taken away to her cell. Her long, shining hair was mussed, her elegant head cover had slipped down to her shoulders, and her face was swollen. Like a mischievous child who manages to do exactly what she wants despite the disapproval of adults, she turned to me and smiled. At that moment I had understood something she had told me about the patience of the Bedouin.

The Bedouin waits forty years for revenge, and when he gets it, he says, "Why was I in such a hurry?"

Um Athaba's husband had beaten and imprisoned her in their home. One night she had burned her husband to death while he slept.

December 17

The day's languid hours meandered through our cells; the monotony and boredom met no resistance from our minds and bodies. Was there any meaning to our teetering on the edge of oblivion? The prisoners already sentenced knew what wait was left for them—months, years—as they eagerly counted the passing days. I was awaiting a different kind of fate. With nothing to guide me except a faint light filtering through the bars, my nights were consumed by insomnia and worry. Owing to fatigue, I trained my mind to relish daydreams;

then I developed a technique to dream I was asleep. I dreamed that I took Um Jassim's sleeping pills. I dreamed that I lost consciousness, was transferred to the hospital. I dreamed of my inmate friends' panic and fear for my life. I dreamed . . . I saw . . . .

# ORDINARY DREAMS

Each night, after her hot bath, she throws her body on the bed and waits patiently for sleep. Following a long, exhausting day, her body has very simple demands: to be embraced by the coma of warm sleep, to be visited by dreams. Still, her mind is alert. She files the day's events in the cabinets of her memory. Each cabinet sits on a shelf. The shelves are the various parts of her body. She rests her head on the pillow. She relaxes for minutes on end, preferring to sleep on her back after covering her head with her duvet. She feels suffocated, pushes the duvet away to breathe. She turns onto her left side, onto her back, then onto her stomach. She stops trying so hard and looks at the alarm clock. Tick, tock. The night hours are slow walkers, enjoying the darkness. Tick, tock. One second after the other. The hours chew the minutes, the minutes chew the seconds. She sits up, leans on the pillow to watch the night with its wide-open mouth. When she asked her doctor for sleeping pills, he said insomnia is a psychiatric condition. The best way to deal with it is to ignore it. When will the windmill of her mind stop turning? What can she do with a body that moans whenever she moves and refuses to take the doctor's advice?

What about the whirling problems, her endless thoughts, the tedious noise of memory, the familiar voices that shroud her nights?

She was doomed to hear them, to stop listening to herself. How many times has she listened to her own voice, replied silently to herself without the courage to respond aloud? She was not interested in the person talking to her, despite her attentiveness, preferring rather to hear other sounds: the ripple of water, the playful cries of children throwing stones into a river, the contented singing of a man in the distance. Tick, tock. She thinks about the future, coming events, and her longing mixed with fear, guilt, and failure. What will happen when she goes back to her city? Will the others deny her presence? She looks and sees herself as a stranger arriving in the city for the first time. Pale, she stands among them. Her city is like she is, deserted but crowded with strangers. It looks with its lonely eye at its dying sons; the other eye had been gouged out by fear. Violently, she thrusts out a fist, as if trying to rid herself of a spider's web that is in the way. Here is the dawn, covering her with its hollow dome. Tick, tock. The whirl of a mind as it moves away. The mind slows its pace.

Fatigued, it returns to the body to accompany it on its tardy voyage of sleep. She cuddles sleep and sings her lullaby of the future. Perhaps she will be able to touch the blue of the sky. Perhaps she will attain depths of joy. Maybe she will find what she has been looking for. Maybe she will reach the merciful dawn. The dead might forgive the living and be liberated from their eternal insomnia. Perhaps she will find the dead awaiting her so they might travel together.

Dream One

She was sitting on a wooden chair behind a polished, wooden desk. The chair was nailed to the wall. She opened the right-hand drawer and found a pile of notepads and a pencil. The notepaper was brown, similar to the paper she had used in school. She arranged the pads before her and started writing. She wanted above all to complete the last chapter of the autobiography she had started over three years ago. Before writing the first words, she looked around her. Opposite was a large window overlooking a calm landscape. To her right was a wall covered in pictures, none of which claimed her attention. Before looking to her left, she began writing. She sighed and quietly sang a folk song she had forgotten years ago. Her heart pounded with joy. She scolded herself for being so lazy, for postponing her writing for so long. The pencil moved faster and faster. Page after page, words, sentences, paragraphs. She traveled far from the present to remote lands. The sound of the past became as loud as the present. She was writing nonstop now. She mingled with her words, describing the old city, the mountains, valleys, and villages of her childhood. A journey aimed at satisfying her thirst for streams of cold water in summer, a journey of sheer pleasure, the long, slow touch of fingers wandering aimlessly over a sleeping body in the early morning, revealing the land of plenty. That remote place of dreams mixed with dreams, that world she was trying to capture in words, would soon be read by others, who would ask her, Did these things really happen? Her reply would be a mysterious nod of the head. Suddenly she felt something take hold of her, transporting her back to the nailed chair, the polished desk, the unfamiliar room. Like a soul plunged in deep sleep who awakes suddenly to find someone watching, she awoke from her writing and found a man sitting behind her. He wasn't there before, she said to herself. She looked around her once more. There were slight changes in the place.

She was sitting behind a wooden desk on a chair nailed to the wall in a corridor whose tiled floor was exactly like the yard in her family's home in Baghdad. Three yards to her right, there was an old door decorated in Arabic script and brass. Ah, it was the door to the public baths she had frequented since the age of five. She had gone then to Kirkuk to stay with some old relatives. Despite her tears, Aiasha, her father's great aunt, had insisted on taking her to the bathroom since they did not have their own. Aiasha, frail but determined, found it hard to open the heavy door and kept pushing until they were inside a dark passageway. The door seemed as if it were part of the wall. Facing her, the man sat smiling, his eyes gleaming with contentment, his face relaxed. Behind him there were two windows that opened onto a small yard surrounded by a high wall. Where was the calm landscape? She avoided looking at him and turned to her left. The corridor was empty. The place resembled a convent. At that moment a priest came by, his head bent, staring eagerly at the floor. She could not see his face. Her one concern was to avoid the stranger's presence. With an exaggerated gesture, she began tidying up papers. She was shocked at the amount she had written, dozens of pages. She was confused. Why was he watching her? Why did he not stop smiling?

To occupy herself, she began numbering the pages before her. She accepted the fact that she had written them. But how to avoid the benign face, the watchful eyes? Was he smiling because he had read her manuscript? She could not move from her seat. She did not have the courage to look into his eyes. Suddenly, the door opened; dust particles filled the air, swirling up and down in the sun's rays. A big man, wearing a white shirt and navy blue trousers, appeared. His face was familiar: she must know him! The fat, heavy face exchanged a laugh with the other man. He glanced over her gloomily, as if she did not exist. He looked at the man to her left. "It must be a nightmare," she thought. "Soon, I'll wake up. This man was not here before. Where did he come from?"

He was seated on a wooden bench that looked as if it had just come from a park, his head in his hands. The bench was covered in moss. From where she sat, she could smell the peculiar scent of damp wood mingled with the sweat of terrified bodies. The big man nodded to the sitter to follow him. He managed with difficulty to lift himself from the bench, his features contorted with pain. Again, slowly, he disappeared through the door. A few minutes later, the silence was shattered by a continual scream of pain. It was only then that she realized what was going to happen. Her turn was next. The same big man would soon return to take her away. What was she doing there? What about the stack of papers? Amid her panic, she noticed that she had written about a hundred pages. Had she written anything against the regime? Had she mentioned her comrades' names? What about her family? She calmed herself. She would find some-where to hide these pages. She would find a way to get rid of them. She gathered up the pages and tried to hide them among the notepads, but all the pads were covered in her handwriting. She looked to the right and left. She looked at the door, then at the man and the corridor. Her heart thumped painfully. She wanted to move, but her chair was nailed to the wall. How could she avoid provok-ing the man's anger? A cold sweat ran down her back and legs. She was suffocating: how difficult it was to breathe! Her bones groaned. Fear rose in her body like liquid in a test tube. She anticipated torture, humiliation and . . . that scream, would it never stop!

For a few minutes, darkness held sway. She touched her forehead. It was wet, as was her hair. She embraced the notepads, but their number was increasing by the minute. She looked at the man, wishing he would disappear, or that at least his smile would fade. It was very cold. There was a draft emanating from the wall. She started to shiver violently . . .

Dream Two
She awoke to find herself with her family, with her deceased father and mother. Both had died four years before. Her grandmother sat there with Aunt Layla and all her cousins. Husbands, wives, and children. It seemed as though they had gathered to welcome her back after years of absence. They were in her family's sitting room. The room was tidy, the way she had left it the day she departed, swearing never to return until there was a change of regime. The television set still dominated the

room. On the sofa opposite sat her father as usual, watching the news and cursing at what he saw. At that moment she remembered she had forgotten to bring them presents, especially something for her father and mother.

All of them were asking her in a babble of voices about her life abroad, her work and friends, about life in the other city. They could not stop questioning her. In that happy atmosphere, she realized that her father was silent, that her mother sat in a corner knitting, looking at her between stitches but remaining quiet. Her large eyes conveyed blame and censure. She went and sat next to her mother and said, "Mother, I wish you could visit me in my flat. I've furnished it the way you like. I'm much better off than before. I've waited so long for you to come. I've saved my holidays, thinking that I'd rather spend them with you."

Her mother remained silent, and carried on knitting as she stared back. Why did they refuse to speak to her? Why did they look at her with such resentment and blame? In her father's eyes, she beheld the dream so often repeated in front of her: "I see her a short distance off from me, vomiting blood. I can't approach her to help. I can't move. I'm unable to do anything. I can see her before me, dying, soaked in her own blood."

The voices became louder, the voices of her grandmother, aunts, and cousins. The room grew vast to accommodate all these people. She was far away, trying helplessly to reach her father and mother, to kiss her father, to touch them both, talk to them, to tell them how much better she understood them now, how she missed them!

Dream Three

It was after midnight. She deeply inhaled the fresh air, scented with roses, carnations, and irises. She looked up at the clear sky, printed with stars. That was the Great Bear. When was the last time she had seen the stars clearly? Stars and one cloud. She watched the cloud change its shape: it was a child's face. No, it was a tree. A girl skipping from one cloud to another. Or was it the cloud itself, jumping from one sky to another, disguised so as to cheat the wind?

She was happy, delighted by the sky and its glowing stars, especially after having lived for years under a gray sky made up of fog and heavy clouds. The kind of sky that sent you rushing home to get out of the cold. She strolled towards her old home. She wanted the minutes to become hours so she might devour these little pleasures. She had no need of a map: her delighted heart would lead her to the street she wanted. Here is Baghdad's main street, with its columns, two-story buildings, and little shops. Here is the main square with its famous mural presiding over the whole city. The square was empty of people and cars, as were the surrounding streets. She walked alone, her steps echoing in the silence. She knew her address; it was not far from where she stood. Should she walk it? It would not take more than twenty minutes. The city seemed in a deep sleep; its silence was mysterious. Carrying her suitcase, she headed towards the north side of the square, away from the main street. Perhaps if she carried on walking in that direction, she would meet someone to ask about the silence; or she might find a taxi. Instead, she found herself in a dark alley, its houses very old, half-ruined. The smell of sewage was unforgettable. She walked faster, trying to reach the end, but she came to another alley similar to the first. It became very windy. Where were the streets leading to her house?

The suitcase, filled with presents for her family, grew heavier, and she began pulling it behind her. The alley was part of an endless web of alleys. She was overcome by an overpowering stench. She covered her nose with one hand and hauled the suitcase with the other. Suddenly, she froze in her tracks: perhaps her family were all dead! Maybe all the inhabitants of the city were dead! Paralyzed, she dropped the suitcase to the ground and began to cry. Cried in a silence that resembled the silence of the alleyway, the streets, the whole city. She cried in her disappointment at the void of the city that had turned into the stinking alleys and cemeteries with low walls. Ruined, neglected cemeteries whose inhabitants were the people of the city. The grass was dry. Dust covered the flowers, dust covered the tombs, dust covered dust. Perhaps if she ran, she would reach her house. She started running. Maybe her family was all right. Run, run . . . faster. Maybe she could save them. If only she could run faster . . .

# SILENCE

It was twenty minutes past eight in the morning. She wore her green coat and scarf. She pulled her collar up and made sure her gloves were in her pocket before locking the door quietly, trying not to disturb her neighbor or her boyfriend, who was in the next room. She walked on tiptoes. Three stairs . . . two . . . then the landing, followed by nine stairs, treading carefully before closing the front door, again trying her best not to disturb the land- lady, who lived on the ground floor. She picked up the letters—three were addressed to her—and put the rest on the small hall table. She slipped them into her handbag.

In the street she walked as if trying not to dis- turb the whole world, not to wake it up. She began to whisper, instead of talking loudly as she used to in the past. She must walk faster if she wanted to catch the bus. On the way, she met the old woman who lived next door.

"Good morning."

"Is it?"

The usual, welcoming answer! And yet she insisted every morning on uttering the same warm words. The bus stop was at once the first and the last stop. The place where people gathered and drivers took a breather. How she loved it! The place was paved, surrounded by trees and a few small shops. A pharmacy, a bakery, and a grocery store. It seemed like an isolated village; its inhabitants few and its streets and shops even fewer. She looked up, hoping to see the impossible: the sun. The clouds were heavy and it was very cold. Last summer, the place was enchanting. When the sun rose, it had an unusual color, gold mixed with the dew. A dew rising slowly from plants, animals, and human bodies. The color of the gray buildings was transformed. Tense, frozen faces relaxed and seemed to smile.

A wet leaf fell onto her shoulder. Damp weather gave people and places a particular smell, a cold sewer smell. She recalled a painting she had seen recently of a man or maybe a shadow walking down a dark, dusty road. The picture immediately evoked the smell of damp, rotting vegetation. She imagined the growth of moss and ferns. With a short stick, she turned over a stone. Worms scattered, trying to find another refuge. Then she trod on a toadstool. The man in the painting halted and she pulled up short next to him. Through the dense shadows and damp trees with their intertwined branches, a faint light broke through, a light of glowing warmth that transformed the whole landscape—plants, man, and painting. Rain fell. They opened their umbrellas and stood, waiting for the driver to start his engine and open the bus doors for them. She took in the sight of a nearby fence. In summer it was yellow, but in autumn it was repainted green, except for the bottom close to the pavement. Who would give a thought to the bit close to the ground? The color of the pavement was black; the dust was black; the particles of dust in the air were black. When it rained, the black dust would settle on the black pavement, to be mixed with the rotten leaves left over from last autumn, and with tickets and cigarette ends. At last, the double-decker bus doors opened.

It was twenty minutes past eight, and she was still at the end of the line. People grasped their wet umbrellas. The smell of damp, woolen sweaters and coats, folded before they were dry, hung in the air. She did not climb the stairs as usual to take her seat at the top, but stayed downstairs and sat in a back seat next to the window. Like a child, she pressed her nose to the glass, but soon changed her mind. The panes were cold and clouded with people's breath. She needed the presence of others. She wanted to cut through the continual bickering with her boyfriend. The filaments that bound her to herself and her boyfriend were cut now in a few places. As if awakening from a deep coma, she shook her head vigorously and looked around her. The faces were tired. Their voices, if they talked, were resentful. The ghost of work pursued them at night and possessed them during the day. Long-missed havens were far away. Like her, they longed for Fridays. Friday was the dream. She had learned how to exchange the greeting "Thank God it's Friday." No, she would not trade that greeting this coming weekend.

She would not meet him tonight. For the last five years, she had spent her weekdays in a silent dialogue with him, until she met him in his house outside the town. She would sit in the front seat, her back to the other people so nobody would interrupt her daydreams. Why would the woman beside her not stop fidgeting? She was old, in her late sixties, carrying a handmade bag. Her hair was short and her eyes bulbous. Her extraordinary pallor and wrinkled face reminded her of her diabetic father. Perhaps she was diabetic, too. She would not stop fidgeting and kept looking back at the rear window. She put her bag on the seat and then picked it up. She was muttering something.

"Sorry?"

"Have you seen the forty-six bus?"

"No."

The woman got up and made for the door, pressing the bell on the way and gazing at the back window. At the bus stop she did not get off, but stayed where she was, fidgeting irritably. She was tired of watching the old woman and closed her eyes, wishing she were going to bed and not to work.

For years she woke up tired, because she had lain awake most of the night. But last night she had dreamt of a small house built on the edge of a farm. It had one bedroom, a sitting room, kitchen, and a bathroom. The bathroom and toilet were detached. She wanted to go to the toilet, but a stream of people was passing through the farm-yard. Among them, she noticed her father.

He seemed so detached and alone. He did not see her in his solitude. He disappeared behind a pomegranate tree. How she missed him!

She opened her eyes and shook her head, as if ridding herself of dreams, emotions, fatigue, and anguish. Away with all these feelings! She tried to push them behind the roadside trees and traffic lights and lines of people waiting. Waiting for what?

No matter how close, the townspeople's bodies did not radiate warmth. She was dreaming of her old house beneath the stars. Villages of stars, cities of stars. Her house, her home were far away. Here, her room, despite all her efforts to decorate it, was nothing but a small box where she slept, ate, and watched the screen of a smaller box for hours on end.

"In our house, we were . . ." "In our garden, we had . . ." "Most of what we plant bears fruit . . ." "The smallest garden has orange and pomegranate trees." And if he mentioned that here there were many kinds of flowers, she would protest, "But they lack all the perfume of our roses!" In the beginning, he accepted that and seemed enchanted by the tales of her people, her country, and its rich history. He asked her about her family, the customs and habits of her land and . . . and . . . but as time passed, he grew tired of the closed circuit of her past. Her labyrinth led only to the past. She in turn grew tired of explaining it all. Was there a resting place for her?

At the beginning of their affair, she had hung old pictures of her city on the walls, pictures taken years before her birth. And in time, she added them to her store of memories and talked about places as if she had actually seen them. He loved the room. The books on her shelves were about ancient civilizations, especially her country's. Her mother had sent her the handmade carpet, and on the mantelpiece rested a brass coffeepot with its little cups and tray. He said, "I feel as if I'm back in history." What had fascinated him in the beginning later became a burden. He pointed out gently one day, "New books are published every week. Why don't you read something recent?" One day, he told her angrily, "You're living in the past. Aren't you interested in the present? Our present together, our future?" Stung by his anger, she stopped talking.

A new arrival settled among the bus riders. Silence. The two passengers in front whispered in disgust, while the rest of the passengers ignored the drunk's funny faces and gestures. Drunk at nine in the morning! She knew him. Sometimes he stood in the middle of the road and attempted to direct traffic. Other times, he pretended he was an inspector, checking the bus's timetable. That was if he was sober. But when he was drunk he would ignore his duties, happy just to sing, dance, and shout at passersby. Nobody sang along with him or laughed. They politely but coldly ignored him, pretending to be deep in conversation. Some simply stared out the window. She wiped hers. Why were the townspeople so obsessed with shutting their windows and their heavy curtains, even in summertime? What were they afraid of? She felt suffocated. She opened the sliding window. The people at the front turned sharply and fixed their eyes on her, but without doing or saying anything. It must be the fresh air they hated breathing. She smiled at the drunk, and he called her "my beauty" and sang her a song he had once heard children sing, a song about Dublin City and his love for it. She was embarrassed at his show of emotion. The rest of the passengers kept staring in silence. Like them, she now wanted to avoid him. She opened her handbag, pretending she was looking for something.

She found the letters. The first was from her bank manager, reminding her she was overdrawn. The second was from the council regarding her housing problem. They informed her she was still on a very long waiting list. She turned the third one over many times, looking at the stamp and handwriting. Letters from that part of the world were very important to her. It was from a relative who taught in Algeria. "I got your letter a long time ago, but I put off replying until I felt better. During the summer, I went to Morocco, Spain, and France. When I returned, I found a telegram from my family, telling me they were waiting in Prague to see me. I left immediately and stayed with them for a week. Shall I tell you what's happened? Or shall I leave it until you come to see me? Last year, I was on the verge of madness. I don't exactly know why. Buying a car helped a great deal. When I come close to that state now, I drive for thousands of miles. In your letter, you talked about politics, that strange disease. I don't think we'll ever be cured of it. After all, it is a disease we choose. Your exile doesn't mean you've escaped from it. And don't laugh if I say that, despite everything, I'm still optimistic. I try and keep it that way. Of course, when I say that life here is unbearable, I don't want to stop you from coming to visit us. On the contrary, Europeans find this country fascinating. They find here all the romance they're craving. Don't worry about your expenses. I don't think you'll need a lot of money to spend here. They give us lots of *dinars* that we can't even spend. Waiting for your reply. Love . . ."

She felt disoriented. A tiny particle of fear rose up inside her, from the depths of her heart. Fear . . . pain . . . A feeling that grew bigger and bigger, as if to engulf her. She was used to dealing with that feeling. She would enfold her legs in her arms, squat down, and completely isolate herself from voices, faces, and her surroundings. She recognized the symptoms. She must get off the bus. It was quarter past nine. She was late. She looked anxiously through the back window and then at the driver. When would they get to the bus stop? She wanted to squat down on the floor and blot out whatever was going to happen. The bus stopped. She got off. She was late. Instead of going in the usual direction, she crossed the road. The pain increased; acid rose sharply in her stomach. There was a lump in her throat she could not get rid of. She would go back home. She squatted on the pavement. She looked with wide, empty eyes at the uncaring passengers. They did not need her.

# EPILOGUE

During a visit to Tunis in 1999, a friend offered me a set of old issues of *Al-Thawra*, the Iraqi national newspaper. I eagerly leafed through them, as I had had no access to the newspaper since the UN sanctions were imposed on Iraq in 1990. At the bottom of the local news page, within a missing persons ad, I read: "On May 1, 1998, a young man named Haidar, pictured above, left his home in the Al-Salam district, not to be seen since. He is of lean build and average height. If you can help, please contact us at phone numbers [given]. God recompenses and rewards."

At that moment I recalled this name and a certain past event that I had forgotten for over twenty years. Up until then, I thought I had been true to myself and others when I wrote *Dreaming of Baghdad* (originally published as *Through the Vast Halls of Memory* in 1990 in France), into which I very slowly poured the events of my past.

Why had I not written about Haidar? Had I really forgotten about him in the fog of recalling others? Or had I been in denial, trying to rid myself of the memory of his short tragic life, the last chapter of which I had witnessed? Was it my fear of acknowledging what had happened to him that caused such a lapse in memory? Or was it my belief that there would have been no point in opening up such old wounds?

When was Haidar executed? Why was it that I had not missed his presence in Nawchilican, the Communist Party's central leadership base, for months after his disappearance? Had I witnessed his execution myself, or had I only heard of it from others and then kept silent about it?

Writing about memories is an elusive process. It often begins with a good intention: to convey the truth. What happens in reality is that we only write down what passes through the censors' eyes. The censors here are the ambient time and space, social and political conditions, and the psychological changes in the writer herself. What one writes now is certainly not what actually happened. It is but a vague indicator of what might have happened, a mixture of illusive and constructed images, a dream, or an act conditioned by either a denial or a desire to see past events shaped by what is yearned for in the present.

I remember that at that time in the early 1970s, our emotions were buried under the tutelage of ideology. We were far too occupied with the struggle to recognize each other as individuals, to the extent of sometimes failing to behave humanely. We wore the garb of belief, carrying it like an ever-tightening shield to distance ourselves from one another, to avoid disappointment and suffering. We needed to make it easy to get rid of others at the moment we imagined them deviating from the straight and narrow path of our belief.

On a personal level, we did not know love, we did not convey emotions, and we did not know how to be truthful with ourselves and one another. We lived in a state of perpetual fear, fear that we might be betrayed, that one of us would inform on our location when we were arrested and tortured. Or that one of us would confess when caught, then come back and infiltrate us further.

At times it was a desperate, daily struggle for survival. Reflection and self-evaluation on our achievements and failures was a luxury we could not afford. Some days were reduced to a question that weighed like a rock on our chests: Will we remain silent if caught? Will we endure torture without confessing or betraying anyone? Death was the only proof of innocence. To live was evidence of treason, and this assumption had the rule and force of law. No one had ever disputed it.

While fighting the oppressive regime, we, without realizing the gradual change, were putting on, one piece at a time, the garments of the executioner. But we always avoided looking in the mirror. We were exhausted from constant fleeing, changes in hiding places, arguments, fear, doubts, guilt, and worries about our families. I remember when Haidar arrived at the base. He was pale, thin, and nervous. He claimed that he escaped from Baghdad to reach the safety of Nawchilican after his release from Qasr al-Nihaya, where he was detained for three days only. He had no convincing reason for his early release. With him he brought doubt, fear, and the smell of death. His attempts to break the wall of silence surrounding his survival failed. How long did he stay at the base? I didn't want to ask.

Writing about the past is a game the writer plays by feints with memory. She chases them but they slip away and hide in the enigma of time and place, in the labyrinth of the present and the unconsciousness of dreams. Memories are too elusive to grasp as the truth. Some construct them, while others erase them. "I" sometimes becomes all, and everyone else is erased. Truth hides behind layers of colored clouds that filter it and allow only glimpses. The truth is covered, events camouflaged. The writer sees the past, like looking at an old photograph. The photographer is the only one who can freeze memory in an instant. And the photograph belongs to that instant alone. It cannot go beyond that one moment; it shows nothing else. The photograph itself is without memory. At most it can turn into a symbol or a sign at a junction. Who knows, one of those roads may lead to a secret memory covered in time. Memory is multilayered; its architecture varies according to the intentions of the carrier. It is the unwritten record of the past. Its only partner is forgetting.

# AFTERWORD

Haifa Zangana's exquisite text, *Fi Arwiqat Al-Dhakira* (In the Halls of Memory), is beautifully translated from Arabic and rendered as *Dreaming of Baghdad* in this new English-language edition. It is a work about memory and dreaming as much as it is a record of the horrendous experience of incarceration.

This compelling memoir weaves together multiple narrative techniques. As the Moroccan critic Mohammed Berrada has pointed out, it defies genre classification. It is a book that recalls Baghdad by a narrator living in exile, but it is also a set of recollections of time past with occasional sublimities and serial horrors. The original Arabic title recalls Saint Augustine, when he writes in his *Confessions* (10. 8. 14) about *aula ingens memoriae* (the vast hall of memory). *Dreaming of Baghdad* is also a confession of sorts: it admits vulnerability, failure, and loss. It refrains from the standard politicized prison literature that endows the detained with heroic stamina. Under torture the protagonist ends up signing a false statement denouncing herself.

In using the first person and the third person pronouns (I and she) to narrate the self as Zangana does, Saint Augustine's famous words come to mind: "All this I do within myself in the huge hall of my memory. There also I meet myself and recall myself." The doubling of the self into observer and observed takes the shape of a split self, of a shattered self, in Zangana's narrative. Writing becomes both a process of analysis as well as one of healing and soldering.

The richness of the text derives partly from the interface between the personal and the political, and partly from mixing memory with desire. The private is invaded in jail by the political and its repressive mechanisms. The naked body is stripped bare of intimacy when it is displayed publicly unto the gaze of the jailers. But despite the deprivations, moments of bonding with the other female inmates offer a relief in this inferno. Nocturnal interrogations, coerced confessions, and humiliation mentally and physically dehumanize the prisoners. As they scream in horror and pain, the sound becomes akin to the howling of wounded animals.

While Zangana's lived experience in this imaginatively structured memoir can be contextualized—Iraq of the early 1970s and London of the late 1980s—the story goes beyond the circumstantial events of the time to become an existential parable. It is about a young, progressive Iraqi woman set on creating, with her comrades, a free homeland teeming with happy compatriots. Dreams of a better Iraq turn into nightmares of an infernal Iraq.

Set when the Baath regime was in power, when fear was instilled and those opposed were hunted, this work is not simply denouncing a given oppression; it denounces the very notion of oppression. Zangana insists in her prologue that the faces of repression in Iraq have changed but the repression itself remains—foreign occupation or domestic despotism use the same infamous prison, Abu Ghraib, to physically maim and psychologically degrade. The brutalization of human beings is described in an almost neutral tone but with the minute details of an anatomist. Though documentary in essence, Zangana's mode of writing liberates the text from the confines of the specific and globalizes the experience.

Memory is selective and often oxymoronic, combining opposites: the horrors of the past with the joys of bygone times. Within the Kafkesque tableau of Zangana, we encounter early childhood pleasures, humorous teenage camaraderie, and women bonding in jail. The narrative is not linear: it presents vivid scenes of the protagonist's life from the mid 1950s when she was a child to the early 1990s when she is in her early forties. The reminiscences are not chronological. But when all is put together, we have a powerful panorama of Iraqi life over four decades. While politics reigns supreme in the history of these decades, this book also depicts Iraqi culture with its strong family ties, gender relations, and generational conflicts.

*Dreaming of Baghdad* focuses on the author's incarceration in 1972, a year she began as a student at the University of Baghdad. Piecing together the different references and allusions to the historical period, the reader is able to fully appreciate the unfolding narrative. Under the Baath Party regime, the leadership of the Iraqi Communist Party (ICP)—the most influential opposition party since the 1940s—was co-opted into joining the government under the so-called National Front. This deepened the rift in the ICP and some, including the protagonist, continued to struggle against the authorities. The bases of armed opposition were in the marshes in the south of Iraq and in the mountains in the north of Iraq (Iraqi Kurdistan). Coordination, including clandestine communication, was the responsibility of party members in Baghdad. Zangana depicts the youthful idealism of her political pursuits and those of her comrades in Baghdad and in the base in the northern village of Nawchilican—all filtered through the memory of a survivor living in London and experiencing the alienation of an exiled existence.

The remarkable feat of this work is its stylistic economy. In a few narrative strokes we get to know the protagonist, her comrade Fouad, her father, and her fellow women inmates—Um Wahid, Um Jassim, and Um Ali. *Dreaming of Baghdad* opens in epistolary mode, offering both intimacy and a conversational dimension. By reading the letters of a friend sent to the protagonist the reader becomes acquainted with her by overhearing this one side of a conversation. One is never sure if the correspondence is between two friends living in exile or if the addressee, Haifa, is also the addressor. Calling on the narrative techniques of suspense-in-delay and mise en abyme associated with *The Arabian Nights*, the third letter stops short of giving details but promises to do so in the next letter and in it another letter of an exiled Iraqi is embedded.

While the six letters are written from outside of Iraq in the late 1980s when the Iran-Iraq war was raging, the next chapter, "Zino" takes us to a Kurdish village on the Iraqi-Iranian border in the late 1950s. The protagonist's visit with her father to his family presents an ethnographic view of village life couched in pastoral poetics. The mosaic of Iraqi society is displayed in the books and pamphlets on sale in the *Suq* in Arabic, Kurdish, Turkish, and Persian. Seen through the eyes of a child, Zino becomes the protagonist's lost paradise as she matures. In a deliberate shift from the country to the city, the following chapter is about Baghdad, the complex urban metropolis. Here we encounter the protagonist more than a decade later in the prison of Qasr al-Nihaya (literally "The Palace of the End"). As she recalls the myriad ways she was tortured by police officers, Zangana does not lose her sense of irony, noting that her torturers were also tortured and executed later on. The irony is further condensed when Zangana recalls how she first visited this prison house as a child when it was transformed from a royal palace into a palace of the people following the 1958 revolution. Through the dialogue of the child with her grandmother, the author alludes to the violent character of the Iraqi revolution.

The references to detention and torture mentioned in the "Baghdad" chapter are taken up again in the chapter entitled "Qasr al-Nihaya," further elaborating on how the protagonist was forced to sign a pre-composed confession accusing her of joining the Party to pursue libertine pleasures and sexual promiscuity. In "Heart, What Have You Seen?," prison life is further detailed by using diary entries written between August 20 and December 17, 1972, when she was transferred to Abu Ghraib. The protagonist was located in a cell of criminal women next to a cell of prostitutes. The stories of women's miseries and how they ended up in this jail, the small celebrations and the awful tensions, and the bonding and the quarrels all unfold. Even though the women inmates are illiterate, the protagonist sets out to teach them the alphabet and recites to them the most popular Iraqi oppositional poet, Mudhafar Al-Nawab, whose work is described by Barbara Harlow as ". . . manifesto, nursery poem, the voice of the collectivity and an ode to heroism and resistance" (75–76).

From the format of the diaries, Zangana moves to obsessive surrealistic dreams that haunt the protagonist. In the penultimate chapter, "Silence," the author takes us back to London only to show us the wreck of life that the protagonist leads, devoid of joy and preoccupied with the past. Again the epistolary plays a role in the form of a letter from a relative in Algeria. The letters show the collective state of mind of exiled Iraqis, suffering in their out-of-place existence.

The last chapter, entitled "Epilogue," is in fact a rectification. It presents a dramatic and radical twist to the entire work. While all along the reader has been empathizing with the victims whether in jail, in the underground, or in a base outside the reach of the authorities, there is a strong hint here that the victims were in fact, victimizers. This drastic turn takes place in 1999 when the protagonist comes across old issues of *Al-Thawra* newspaper—the official Iraqi newspaper of the Baath Party—announcing a missing young person by the name of Haidar and entreating readers who know of his whereabouts to inform his family. This triggers a flashback in the mind of the protagonist in which a certain Haidar came to join the ICP in the liberated base in northern Iraq after being detained, and was released by the regime after only three days. It is precisely his short detention, the absence of torture on his body, and his joining the base that made his comrades wonder if he had made a deal with the authorities and turned into an informer on them. Survival itself under such circumstances becomes suspect. Zangana hints rather than states in this finale what had happened to Haidar. The Iraqi critic, Salam Ibrahim, interprets the hint to mean that the suspect was executed by his comrades for fear he was an infiltrator. Zangana asks herself why she had repressed his memory all along in her work: "When was Haidar executed? Why was it that I had not missed his presence in Nawchilican . . . Had I witnessed his execution myself or had I only heard of it from others and then kept silent about it?" Here is the ultimate confession freely but belatedly made, giving the work a postmodern flavor.

This memoir is a prime example of a testimonial to be read by human rights activists and psychologists interested in traumatic experiences; it is also a sophisticated literary text using the conscious and the subconscious, dreams and diaries, dialogue and stream of consciousness, crosscutting and embedding to tell a moving story. While the political struggle is the matrix of the narrative, gender issues are the warp and weft of its fabric. The work offers intimate views on a variety of relationships: the demasculinization of the father as a middle-aged patriarch, the sister-keeper role imposed on the big brother, and the gendered stuggles of women. The work narrates women's stories outside prison that led to their incarceration and does not shy away from describing menstrual periods and labor pain, heterosexual longing and same-sex intimacy.

*Dreaming of Baghdad* is indeed a great work of literature articulated from a witness stand. Barred and silenced for a long time, Haifa Zangana uncovers the dynamics of detention and the anguish of surviving the experience.

Ferial J. Ghazoul
Cairo
May 2009

## WORKS CITED

Berrada, Mohammed. "Intisar Al-Kitaba fi Aqbi-
    yat Al-Ta'dhib" (The Triumph of Writing over
    the Dungeons of Torture), *Nour 6* (Winter
    1996): 18–19.

Harlow, Barbara. *Barred: Women, Writing, and Political
    Detention.* Hanover, NH: Wesleyan University
    Press, 1992.

Ibrahim, Salam. Review of *Fi Arwiqat Al-Dhakira*
    (In the Halls of Memory). http://www.ahewar
    .org/debat/show.art.asp?aid=88634

Saint Augustine, *Confessions,* R. S. Pine-Coffin,
    trans. Harmondsworth: Penguin, 1961.

# ACKNOWLEDGMENTS

My heartfelt gratitude is to my editor Amy Scholder who made the new edition of this book possible. For her patience, encouragement, valuable insights, and comments I am truly grateful.

To Peter Wood, the late Surrealist poet and director of Hourglass Press. I am indebted to him for his support a long time ago, for taking the risk to publish a first book by a young Iraqi writer at a time when not many British people knew where Iraq was.